Penguin Crime Fiction
Editor: Julian Symons
By Hook or by Crook

Emma Lathen

By Hook or by Crook

Penguin Books

Penguin Books Ltd, Harmondsworth,
Middlesex, England
Penguin Books, 625 Madison Avenue,
New York, New York 10022, U.S.A.
Penguin Books Australia Ltd, Ringwood,
Victoria, Australia
Penguin Books Canada Ltd, 2801 John Street,
Markham, Ontario, Canada L3R 1B4
Penguin Books (N.Z.) Ltd, 182–190 Wairau Road,
Auckland 10, New Zealand

First published in Great Britain by
Victor Gollancz Ltd, 1975
Published in Penguin Books 1978

Made and printed in Great Britain by
C. Nicholls & Company Ltd,
The Philips Park Press, Manchester
Set in Monotype Times

1. A Loaf of Bread Beneath the Bough

Wall Street is a great repository. Gold, bonds and packets of thousand-dollar bills nestle in steel-lined vaults; armed guards protect everything from diamonds to sacred relics. Deep underground there are caverns rivaling those of Ali Baba.

But stacks of short-term Treasuries below the asphalt are the least of Wall Street's responsibilities. It is the intangibles that cause all the trouble. Clipped coupons and tendered warrants are not the only things that wing their way to lower Manhattan like swallows *en route* to Capistrano. There are also hopes and dreams. Unlikely as it may seem, Wall Street is the lodestar for some of the nation's most cherished myths.

Year in, year out, the Sloan Guaranty Trust gets more than its share of the prevailing illusions. Each Christmas brings news of light bulbs that never burn out and of sinister industrial barons withholding them from the public. During the long icy grip of winter the barons reappear frequently, hiding stockings that never sag, destroying engines that operate on rainwater and suppressing grass that never needs mowing. Springtime regularly produces a different cast of phantoms – the men who invest for the Rothschilds, the men who invest for the Vatican and the men who invest for the Mafia. Nowadays, since the Sloan is the third largest bank in the world, there are beginning to be tales about the men who invest for the Kremlin.

But summer is the cruelest season. Every steamy July day some well-heeled innocent is vouchsafed the Delphic vision that there is only one place to put his money. It may be in gold coins, or in real estate or in Jackson Pollocks. But, as John Putman Thatcher had learned long before he became senior vice-president of the Sloan Guaranty Trust, never – never in a bank.

This year there was a new twist, as Thatcher discovered during lunch with three of his subordinates from the Trust Department. A heat wave had kept him in the building. He had been in the elevator before he remembered that Con Edison was not simply skipping dividends. Its latest brownout had forced certain housekeeping economies at the Sloan. The Executive Dining Room was no longer airconditioned. Ten minutes later he had a loaded tray in his hands and was reconnoitering the Employees' Cafeteria. When he reached his table, he was not surprised to find Everett Gabler, his oldest and most cantankerous colleague, in the midst of complaint.

'I explained very carefully to Wentworth that rare books are a desirable investment only if you have expert knowledge of rare books.' Gabler quaffed his buttermilk, set the empty glass down on the Formica tabletop and continued: 'Otherwise it is the height of folly to suggest liquidating a sound, diversified portfolio which is outperforming the market. Unless, of coure, you want to make some book dealer rich!'

Kenneth Nicolls, a junior trust officer, ventured to reply: 'A lot of people seem to enjoy collecting first editions.'

'Enjoy? What does enjoyment have to do with maintaining an estate?' Gabler demanded. 'And not only does he propose buying hundreds of first editions; he wants to do it in a rush so that he can leave on one of those interminable trips of his.'

Charlie Trinkam, Thatcher's second-in-command, automatically looked for the silver lining. 'If he doesn't know beans about books, he's going to lose his shirt, no matter how much time he takes. So why not get the agony over with?'

This contribution was ignored. Gabler never made the best of anything. 'And once Kimball Wentworth has disappeared into India,' he predicted starkly, 'we can look forward to hysterical emergency pleas for funds. Why he finds it impossible to make arrangements to collect his quarterly check on a rational basis – '

'The only Wentworth who found it at all possible to make rational arrangements,' Thatcher interrupted, 'was old J.B. Everybody who got cut into his trust fund has been virtually witless.'

Gabler did not waste time contesting this patent truth. Instead, he shifted ground slightly. 'Furthermore, I fail to see the necessity for these endless treks into the unknown. They simply compound our difficulties. Before we know it, we'll be landed with an impostor.'

Inviting Charlie Trinkam to exercise his erratic imagination was always a mistake. 'You mean years from now, the offspring of some beautiful Sherpa is going to turn up claiming to be the legitimate descendant of old J.B.? Come off it, Everett, you've forgotten what Kimball Wentworth is like. Besides, that sort of thing doesn't happen anymore.'

'It would be almost impossible in the modern world, wouldn't it?' Ken Nicolls suggested diffidently.

'You bet it would,' agreed Charlie. 'Hell, they probably have social security numbers in Nepal by now.'

A thin smile of triumph creased Everett Gabler's lips. 'Would it interest you to learn that there is a question of disputed identity on my desk at this very moment?' he asked.

'Good God!' Thatcher was startled enough to abandon the roast beef sandwich that had been claiming most of his attention. 'I don't believe we've had a case like that for over fifteen years.'

Any reference to the Sloan's history had a mellowing effect on Gabler. 'Yes, indeed,' he said warmly. 'But if you examine the files, you'll find the bank had quite a rash of them in the twenties.'

Thatcher nodded. He was familiar with those files. 'In those days everyone seemed to think he could establish a claim on the original Astor or Vanderbilt or Du Pont.'

'And the beauty of it, from their point of view, was the accretion,' said Charlie enthusiastically. 'If they could prove they were entitled to just one founder's share of Union Pacific, then they had coming to them not only the original share and its dividends but also every single penny generated by those profits since the year one. Some of those snowballs amounted to millions.'

Kenneth Nicolls stirred restively. For budgetary reasons, he ate in the cafeteria at least once a week, and usually twice. It was bad enough to be caught at it. But now apparently he was stuck with three superiors mooning over the golden past. What was so wonderful about a lot of fraudulent claims anyway?

'They didn't get away with it, did they?' he asked.

'Most of them didn't even have the rudiments of a case,' Thatcher admitted. 'And you're perfectly right that it was easier in the days before birth certificates and drivers' licenses.'

'Well, whoever he is, this late bloomer has picked the wrong man to tangle with,' Charlie said generously. 'Everett will have this phoney out on his backside within ten minutes.'

Gabler was not grateful for the compliment. On the contrary, he was reproachful. 'Mrs Aratounian is almost certainly not a phoney,' he declared.

His audience came back to earth with a thump.

'Now, wait a minute, Ev,' Charlie protested. 'You were the one who said you had an impostor on your hands.'

'Never mind that,' Thatcher said. 'Since when have the Aratounians been one of America's fine old fortunes?'

Gabler struck back in his own fashion. 'Perhaps you will allow me to explain,' he said, polishing his glasses meticulously. 'I assume you are familiar with the firm of Parajians, Incorporated?'

Charlie Trinkam sucked in his breath sharply. Parajians was the largest Oriental-rug business in the country. Aside from operating as a wholesaler, it maintained sumptuous retail establishments in New York, Dallas, San Francisco and, most recently, Honolulu. Only an idiot could handle the affairs of New York's wealthiest families and remain ignorant of the firm.

'Yes, Everett,' Thatcher said with commendable self-control. 'I believe I have heard the name.'

'How did you get mixed up with them?' Charlie growled.

'The account first came into my hands shortly after I joined the bank,' said Everett with the affection he accorded any event at least thirty years old. 'Originally there had been three Parajians – '

But Charlie Trinkam could take just so much of the stately manner. 'What do you mean – three?' he disputed. 'I always thought that business was a one-man show. In fact, I thought its real name was Paul Parajian, Inc.'

Gabler simply spoke more distinctly. 'Originally, there were three Parajians. The eldest was a daughter who married and moved from Greece to Soviet Armenia, a Mrs Veron Aratounian. The elder boy, Paul, was left a young widower in 1935 and he came to the United States. He took all sorts of odd jobs, pinching and saving to buy a rug every now and then. You're right, Charlie, basically it was a one-man business – with Paul as sole owner and employee. But for a few years he did have his younger brother working for him, and Paul gave him fifteen percent of the stock. When the boy, Haig, was killed in a streetcar accident in 1939, he left the stock to his sister, Veron.'

'In 1939, you say?' Thatcher could see what was coming. 'And in September of that year, Europe was engulfed by war.'

'Precisely. Almost my first duty at the Sloan was communicating with Mrs Aratounian. Heavens, what a time we had!' There was a nostalgic gleam in Gabler's eye. 'Remember, diplomatic relations with Russia had been reestablished only a few years earlier. The Aratounians had moved from their last address. Between completing probate and shipping documents back and forth, we were barely in time.'

Gabler leaned back as if still moved at the thought of that hectic race he had run many years ago.

'In time for what?' Nicolls blurted.

All three of his seniors stared at him in rebuke.

'In time to establish a trust before Russia was sucked into the war too,' Everett snapped with a return to his normal testiness. 'Good God, what do you think our department exists for? Her stock has been held in trust for her by the Sloan ever since. Then came the war and the Cold War, and contact was lost. But for the last twenty years Paul has been exchanging letters with her. Last month he was astonished to learn that his sister was in Teheran planning to come to New York.'

Charlie Trinkam was counting off decades on his fingers. 'Let's see, it's over forty years since they met. Is that what has Parajian worried? I don't see that it's such a big deal if they've kept in touch.'

'To be accurate, they have not met since 1930. But Paul Parajian is not worried. Veron now has no living relatives in the Soviet Union, and Parajian was going to suggest that she move here himself. The only reason he was surprised was that she didn't give him any advance warning.'

'Then,' Thatcher mused, 'I fail to see the problem. Mrs

Aratounian is not the unknown offspring of an unknown marriage. Why the cry of foul play?'

Gabler looked sterner than ever. 'I fear there is dissension in the Parajian family.' A lifetime spent in trusts had exposed him to every variety of family discord, but his disapproval never abated. 'Paul Parajian has four children in all. The three by his first marriage are now adults, and over the years he has been foolishly generous to them with gifts of stock. They now own over forty percent and are conspiring to oust their father from the firm.'

'A classic confrontation.' Thatcher steepled his fingers and nodded gently. 'I assume the Sloan has never voted the trust shares, so that the company has been run on eighty-five percent of its stock. And into this nicely balanced picture comes the missing sister ready to swing an additional fifteen percent to her brother's side.'

Gabler permitted himself a small shrug. 'The children claim that it's too convenient. They say their father was having trouble maintaining his control; their father might have been forced out of active management, and presto! Their father produces an ally – an ally for whom nobody can vouch except himself.'

'Incidentally, what about the fourth child?'

'He's still a schoolboy. You can forget about him.' Gabler hesitated, then decided there was a flaw in his previous testimony. 'Nor are the other three entirely unanimous. The introduction of Mrs Aratounian has thrown them into disarray.'

'I'll bet it has!' Charlie Trinkam snorted jovially. 'After all, it's one thing to claim your old man is past it. It's another thing to accuse him of being a crook.'

Ordinarily this kind of language in connection with a Sloan client would have drawn instant rebuke. But today Gabler seemed forced into reluctant concurrence.

'I doubt if the children themselves would have brought such a charge,' he said. 'Unfortunately, the ringleader of the opposition is Mrs Lois Parajian, the wife of the younger son, Gregory. Her position is hard as rock: The Mrs Aratounian who arrived at Kennedy Airport this morning is an impostor. Paul Parajian is deliberately committing fraud, and she will go to court to prevent any transfer of the fifteen percent.'

'Tell me,' asked Thatcher with genuine interest, 'does Mrs Parajian advance any support for her thesis?'

'Bah! Her mind does not work that way. She simply decides what result will be most advantageous to herself and then she twists ... Yes, what is it?'

The busboy hovering at his elbow announced that there was a call for Mr Everett Gabler and was he sitting at this table?

As Gabler was led off to a wall telephone near the steam table, Thatcher reflected that this was the first amenity of the cafeteria to fall short of those in the Executive Dining Room. Down here the sandwiches were thicker and the iced coffee colder. But upstairs a soft-footed hostess would have wafted Gabler into a private cubicle with a chair and a writing table.

Charlie Trinkam echoed his approval. 'You know, we should eat here more often.'

Before Thatcher could determine whether this was a tribute to the mixed cold plate or further proof of Charlie's inclination for any environment with a healthy leavening of feminine participants, Gabler was back brimming with news.

'That was Paul Parajian,' he said. 'They want to move up their appointment with me and come in this afternoon.'

'Who wants?' Thatcher asked acutely. 'Lois Parajian?'

'No.' Everett was purring with satisfaction. 'It is Mrs Aratounian herself who wants to get things settled, once and for all. Apparently in the teeth of some resistance.'

'It sounds as if the old girl is sure of her case,' Charlie remarked.

Gabler became militant. 'If I find – as I fully expect to – that there is not a vestige of support for Mrs Parajian's irresponsible accusations, I shall make it very clear to her that the Sloan will not lend itself to the needless harassment of an aged lady simply to further Mrs Parajian's selfish goals.'

'I was right all along,' Charlie murmured. 'I was just wrong about whose backside was going to land outside the door.'

Everett was too uplifted to be diverted. 'And now, if you will excuse me, I must review my files. They'll be here as soon as they finish a family lunch they're all having.'

With a spring in his step and a ramrod in his back, he marched to the exit.

Ken Nicolls had been a fascinated observer. 'He really is all worked up, isn't he?'

'All he needs is a suit of armor and a lance,' said Charlie.

Noticing the younger man's confusion, Thatcher explained: 'Everett genuinely enjoys certain forms of combat. And it looks as if he may get his fill this afternoon.'

'Oh, I don't know about that,' Charlie disagreed. 'The fireworks may be over before then. That must be some family lunch they're having!'

2. Come, Fill the Cup

The lunch held in Paul Parajian's apartment high over the East Sixties could have been a lot worse. Language barriers were saving the day. Mrs Veron Aratounian did not speak English, and Mrs Gregory Parajian, née Turnbull, did not understand Armenian. Several sighs of relief had greeted this fortunate dovetailing.

Lois had reacted differently. 'Imagine trying to pass herself off as Paul's sister,' she had hissed to her neighbor early in the game. 'Why, the woman doesn't even know English!'

The reminder that Mrs Aratounian had spent her adult life in Russia, instead of New York, made no impact. And two hours of listening to great torrents of Armenian, with only snippets of translation, merely confirmed her suspicions.

'Why don't they find out how she claims to have gotten to Teheran?' she kept repeating. 'Why don't they pin her down, instead of letting her ask all the questions? Oh, for heaven's sake, what are they talking about now?'

Her last exclamation had been prompted by the loud clucks of dismay Mrs Aratounian was beaming in her direction. The English rendition was not calculated to soothe.

'The old lady just asked how many sons you have. Gregory is explaining about your two daughters.'

'What business is that of hers?' Lois flashed back in a furious undertone. 'She has no right to pry into my affairs.'

'Well, we did agree that we were going to treat this as an ordinary family get-together, didn't we? It's only natural that she wants to catch up on everybody.'

Lois was momentarily deflected. 'Then she can't think much of you and Sara. You don't have any children at all.'

'Oh, she doesn't care about Sara,' Alex Daniels replied cheerfully. 'It's the Parajian name that's important. We don't count for those purposes.'

Alex was a tall, stooped man, distinguished by thick horn-rimmed glasses and a taste for mildly malicious comment. He had always gotten along well with his wife's father and brothers. But from the day of Gregory's engagement, he had adopted a policy of unswerving hostility toward Lois. He disliked her attempts to patronize his wife, he disapproved her ruthless management of her husband and, above all, he was affronted by her silent assumption that the two of them shared a common bond of superiority. She was influenced, he supposed, by the fact that he called himself Daniels instead of Danielian, by the fact that he had attended Yale and by the fact that he played squash. There was very little he could do about this – although strongly tempted to change his name back – but he never missed an opportunity to contradict Lois as flatly as possible.

'You see,' he continued, pointing down the table, 'now she's asking about Mark's children.'

There was little need for the comment. Mrs Aratounian was nodding vast approval. Mark, her elder nephew, not only had three young sons but had a daughter already planning her wedding.

'I thought even peasants had gotten past that way of thinking,' Lois said with disdain. 'This whole affair is being mismanaged. I warned Gregory how it would be, but he's so soft he'll do anything to avoid unpleasantness.'

'I've noticed,' Alex said smoothly.

As usual, his barb bounced off Lois' armor. 'Things would be different if I were next to that woman,' she muttered.

It was this very consideration that had led to Harriet Parajian's seating arrangements. Left to his own devices, her husband, Paul, would have carelessly swept everyone into the dining room without a thought for the consequences. Harriet had firmly exercised her prerogatives as hostess. Mrs Aratounian was flanked by her two nephews, while across the way Paul balanced his daughter, Sara, and Mark's wife, Helen. If challenged, Harriet could have listed excellent reasons for relegating her other guests to the foot of the table.

Barney Olender had worked for Paul so long that he was practically a member of the family, but like Lois, he was not Armenian. Opposite him was Hector Khassim, who had accompanied Veron from Teheran and was here today primarily in his role of courier. And Alex, as he himself acknowledged, was not really a Parajian for purposes of this reunion. But Harriet, and each of the men, knew that their principal function was to act as buffer between Lois and Mrs Aratounian. And they had all done yeoman service.

Immediately upon being seated, Barney and Khassim had started a rapid cross fire about the Oriental-rug business that was as effective as a fence across the table. And Alex, after one resigned look, saw that today he was assigned to bear the brunt. Only a sympathetic glance from his wife sustained him. He was ruefully grinning at her when he suddenly noticed that Sara, the one Parajian of her generation to look conspicuously Armenian, was an unmistakable younger edition of her aunt. Drawing this resemblance to Lois' attention was going to make up for a lot.

But Lois never needed help in finding irritants. 'What in the world is she up to now? Why is she pawing Gregory?'

The tone, more than the words, made Daniels swing around. Mrs Aratounian had pushed aside her plate and was fondling one of her nephew's hands. 'She's just noticed that Gregory is left-handed, that's all,' Alex explained.

'My God, why can't she leave him alone!'

Alex looked at Lois curiously. If there was one thing that normally characterized his sister-in-law, it was her lack of heat. Childlike in her self-absorption, she was almost inhumanly unresponsive to others. But Mrs Aratounian, Daniels noted, had managed to penetrate. Lois was literally crawling with dislike – squirming in her chair, unable to take her eyes off the old lady.

'What's she saying now?' Lois whispered venomously.

'Nothing very important.' Alex was deliberately unhelpful.

'Yes, but what?' Lois insisted.

'She says there's a leftie in every generation and the thing to do is root it out early.'

'That shows how little she knows,' Lois spat. 'The pediatrician told me the other day not to try and interfere with Isobel.'

The pediatrician, thought Alex, was merely the latest in a long line of men urging Lois not to interfere. Poor little Isobel was probably going around with her left arm strapped to her side.

'Well, Veron is admitting that all that nagging and slapping doesn't seem to have done much good. She says there's an old Armenian proverb – like parent, like child.'

'Isobel,' said Lois icily, 'takes after my family'.

She had forgotten to keep her voice lowered, and Hector Khassim, overhearing, could not let this occasion for gallantry pass.

'If your daughter is as beautiful as her mother, then she is indeed fortunate.'

The compliment misfired. By any standards Lois, with her Nordic fairness and slim elegance, was a handsome woman. And she knew it. But, in her opinion, Hector Khassim had no right to say so.

Barney Olender was a man who liked to jolly his way past life's small difficulties. Ignoring Lois' expression, he burbled: 'That's the great thing about families. You have your differences, but you can always put them aside to have a good time. Look at how thrilled everybody is just to be together again. Your Aunt Veron is beside herself. And I've never seen Paul happier.'

This was testimony to the goodness of his heart, if not his eyesight. Veron Aratounian predictably wanted to know all about the forthcoming wedding. Eagerly she was extracting facts about the groom, his family, the bridesmaids, and greeting each detail with a cry of pleasure. But Paul Parajian had drawn his chair slightly aside. Absently toying with his wineglass, he was simply letting the women have their day.

'It's disgusting! Paul's forcing that woman on us,' Lois exploded.

'We all agreed that this was not the time or place to raise challenges,' Alex reminded her.

'I'm not sure this isn't exactly the right time. The longer we delay – '

'We agreed – and for a price,' Alex cut her off.

Barney, horrified by this injection of the seamy side of family life, took refuge in a discussion of reweaving borders with Hector Khassim.

Lois never noticed they were gone. 'It's one thing not to make accusations, but that doesn't mean we have to accept her as Veron. I still don't see why they rushed up and kissed her,' she said, reverting to an earlier complaint.

'I'm sure you don't,' Daniels mocked.

To the credit of the younger Parajians, they had not hung back when an elderly woman tottered into view, still flustered from her long flight, but with her arms stretched wide and her eyes bright with anticipation. Mark had been the first to envelop her in a bear hug, and his brother and sister had followed suit. The initial encounter had set the tone for the ensuing rounds of toasts and family gossip. Paul Parajian had every right to be satisfied with his celebration.

If anything, his sister was now more happily excited than when she had arrived. All her responses were magnified by the emotion of the moment. Laughter and tears had merged continually through the meal. She had started to chuckle at a mild pleasantry by Mark and ended up clutching her side. Almost any sentence she began ended in gasping, incoherent statements of joy. She was flushed with pleasure as she announced her intentions for the rest of the day.

'That's ridiculous,' Lois snapped when Alex Daniels translated.

She was not the only one to object.

'But Paul,' protested Harriet Parajian, following her husband to the phone, 'I don't think it's at all wise to take Veron over to the Sloan now. She's overtired. Why don't you just keep the original appointment you made for tomorrow?'

'Ah!' Paul Parajian gave vent to exasperation, amusement and his own pent-up emotions. 'You heard us, Harriet!'

He was within his rights to say so. For over twenty minutes fully half the table had been pleading and cajoling with Veron.

'She's stubborn,' Parajian said, reaching for the receiver. 'Veron insists that she's already cost me too much. She won't be happy until she has money of her own.'

'Oh, dear,' said Harriet with affectionate commiseration. 'How infuriating – and how like what you would be doing in her place.'

This suggestion arrested Parajian's hand for a moment. Then, with a glint in his eye, he said: 'I suppose you're right. Anyway, don't worry. I'm just going to let Veron hand Gabler whatever identification she's got. Tomorrow will be early enough for all the rest . . . '

He broke off, glanced over Harriet's shoulder, then deliberately resumed dialing. Harriet turned to deal with her guests. First to leave the dining room was not, as she had feared, Lois.

'Barney,' she said gratefully, moving to his side. 'Thank you so much for coming. I'm afraid you've been left out of things.'

Barney had no opportunity to respond with his own particular brand of chipper optimism.

'But we won't hold you up much longer,' Paul interposed, his call finished. 'I'm taking Veron down to the bank right now. I think Sara's coming with us.'

His wife's tiny frown did not escape him any more than Olender's flicker of appraisal.

'Don't worry,' Parajian said loudly enough to be heard by anyone who cared to listen. 'Lois – and everybody else who wants to – can have their innings tomorrow.'

Of course, they did not start immediately. Like all family operations, the Parajian descent on the Sloan was delayed by farewells, searching for coats and handbags, reminders, instructions, advice. In fact, they delayed long enough so that John Thatcher was not only back from lunch but late for his appointment at the Federal Reserve. He was in the elevator when Billings opened the doors, to reveal an astonishing sight in the huge foyer of the Sloan Guaranty Trust.

Instead of the usual roar from a hurrying crowd, there was total, eerie silence. At least fifty people had frozen in their tracks and were staring at a fallen figure. An elderly woman lay stretched out on the marble floor, a doctor kneeling at her side.

Over them stood a man, a younger woman and Everett Gabler.

Gabler did not hesitate. With one step he was at Thatcher's side.

'John,' he said in incredulous outrage, 'the doctor says that Mrs Aratounian has just died.'

3. This Sorry Scheme of Things

John Thatcher was as reverent toward death as the next man, but the Federal Reserve had its claims too. After extending condolences, he proceeded on to his appointment, confident that the Sloan doctor could handle the medical formalities and that Everett Gabler was more than able to deal with the legal problems raised by Mrs Aratounian's passing. It was not until the next morning that his illusions were shattered. Both Dr Bittel and Everett were demanding support.

Gabler was in Thatcher's office before nine o'clock. He rang up the curtain without preliminaries.

'John, I know you have a busy schedule this week. I am sorry to add to your load, but I would like you to make time to see the Parajians.'

Circling his desk, Thatcher raised an eyebrow. One of Gabler's many sterling qualities was his ability to operate independently. When Everett called for help, the wolf was not at the door, he was moving into the guest room.

'Why?' Thatcher asked cautiously. 'I can see that Mrs Aratounian's death is going to muddy the waters further. Somebody should inherit her stock, but with half the family claiming she was an impostor ...' He broke off as Everett coughed sharply.

'I had better bring you abreast of two recent developments,' Gabler said in the voice of doom.

'Perhaps you'd better.'

'Dr Bittel wasn't Mrs Aratounian's doctor, so he couldn't sign a death certificate. But after the ambulance left, he had a word with me in private. John, he says that Mrs Aratounian was poisoned.'

Thatcher resisted the temptation to comment. A fine dramatic instinct always made Everett save his showstoppers for the end. If this was the overture, then the Parajians really were in trouble.

'And this morning,' Everett continued implacably, 'Mrs Lois Parajian telephoned to inform me that Mrs Aratounian's will leaves everything to her nephews and niece. And would I please see that the stock is transferred to the heirs with all possible dispatch.'

Thatcher finally found words. 'If the dead woman was not Mrs Aratounian, there is clearly no estate to distribute.'

For many weeks now, Everett Gabler had been coping with Lois Parajian. He had done so uncomplainingly because it was his duty. But he was not averse to revealing how much he had endured.

'I warned you that she did not have a rational mind. She now claims that there can be no question of an impersonation.'

The response to this simple statement was all that he could have wished.

'Oh, she does, does she?' snarled Thatcher.

'Normally, I would have taken great pleasure in telling her that once such a question had been raised, the Sloan would insist on the fullest investigation. If Mrs Lois Parajian thinks that we are going to follow her lead every time she wishes to reverse her position out of the most transparent avarice,' said Gabler, warming to his theme, 'she is sadly mistaken. Her motives may not be any concern of mine, but that trust fund is. Not one iota of stock will be distributed until I am completely satisfied as to Mrs Aratounian's identity. I will trace every step of her journey from the Soviet Union. I will find out when she left and with whom. I will go back to her birth if necessary!'

Thatcher thanked God that the Cold War was over. On the other hand, could détente survive Everett's Draconic methods? World War III would be a heavy price to pay for these anomalies in the Parajian family.

'Yes, yes,' he said hastily. 'Normally that is what you would have told her, but you did not. Why?'

Everett leaned forward conspiratorially. 'I was not the only one who had a call concerning Mrs Aratounian this morning. The police have asked to see Dr Bittel.'

'Ah!' said Thatcher. 'So Bittel must have been right about poison. Tell me, does this Parajian woman realize that she is giving herself a first-class motive for murder? If the children inherit Mrs Aratounian's stock, they can now take control away from the father.'

'I really do not care,' Gabler said stiffly. 'But I do feel that the family as a whole should be apprised of the Sloan's position. Since I myself am testifying in Boston about the John Hancock building . . .'

Sadly Thatcher let his eye fall on the heavy docket of work his secretary, Miss Corsa, had laid neatly on his desk. He had a feeling that Miss Corsa's hopes for today's output were going to be dashed.

'You're right, of course, Everett. I had better see the Parajians as quickly as possible. But I can't help wondering what the police are making of all this.'

'A real lulu,' said Captain Muller in disgust. 'Where does the old lady drop dead? The Sloan Guaranty Trust, for Christ's sake! Who are the next of kin? The same Parajians who operate on Fifth Avenue. Well, we've had murders in fancy families before. With that much clout around, we should have a bunch of high-priced lawyers telling us that everybody loved the old lady, that she died a natural death or, at worst, it was an accident and they shot her thinking she was a burglar. And, of course, the family's in bed with shock and can't answer any questions. Instead, what do we get?'

His assistant was ready with a list. 'First, the Sloan doctor won't touch the death certificate with a ten-foot pole and shovels the mess into Bellevue. Second, the relatives can't even agree on who the old lady is, in spite of the fact that they've all just come from a party for her. As far as staying in bed goes, they don't have time. They're too busy changing their minds about who the corpse was so they can inherit her bundle. Do you think they're doing everything in the open to convince us they couldn't be murderers?'

'I don't want to know why a bunch of loonies act the way they do,' Captain Muller growled. 'What I want is hard facts. What have we got?'

The third man in the room removed his spectacles and pushed aside the report he had been studying. 'Quite a lot,' he said. 'It's an open-and-shut case. There's no doubt about the time of death. So far, the pathologist says the poison was one of the nitrites, probably amyl nitrite or nitroglycerin. She must have ingested the stuff two to four hours before death. We were lucky about the stewardesses on the flight from Iran. They hadn't started back yet. They swear that the old lady didn't have anything yesterday morning on the plane. And the only thing she had to drink was water from the same cooler everybody else used.'

The assistant gave a grunt. 'That makes it tighter than a drum. She got the stuff at this party.'

'Wait a minute,' Muller interrupted. 'What does the pathologist say about symptoms of nitrite poisoning?'

'Headache, dizziness, tremors, pallor, violent then diminished heart action. Death in this case from cardiac failure.'

'Well, that's the first thing that Parajian bunch can explain to me.' Captain Muller was levering himself upright. 'For two hours she had those symptoms in the middle of her ever-loving family. Why didn't they call a doctor instead of running off to a bank?'

'You've got enough to lean on them.'

Muller shook his head. 'Oh no, I want more before I tackle them. After all, there were two people at that lunch who didn't stand to gain or lose a thing by Mrs Aratounian's death. Why did they stand around and watch her die?'

'You've got it all wrong,' Barney Olender protested when they tracked him down at Parajians. 'You don't understand.'

Captain Muller was remorseless. 'I understand she was an old lady in a strange country. You were the only people she could turn to. Maybe you didn't realize she was dying, but you could see she was sick. And you didn't do anything about it.'

The heavy accusing tone had rattled Olender. 'She was sick when she got off the plane,' he blurted.

'That won't get you anywhere. We've got plenty of witnesses to prove she wasn't poisoned on the plane.'

'That's not what I mean!' Barney was shouting his denials now. Suddenly he subsided, producing a handkerchief to mop his brow. 'Look, will you just let me explain?' he pleaded.

'It's time somebody did.'

Barney took a deep breath. 'I don't know how much you know about the background. Veron Aratounian wasn't in very good shape when she turned up in Teheran a month ago. She had to go into a convalescent home for a while. Sure, she was all right when she got out, but she was still old. And then look at the day she put in. She'd never been on a plane before in her life and she started with a jet trip from Iran to New York. Khassim said she was on the verge of airsickness for hours. He spent most of the trip with his hand on the bag, ready to whip it out for her. On top of that, her ears got blocked up during the descent to JFK. I didn't see her at the airport, but I can tell you what she was like when she showed up at the apartment. She was white and she was dizzy and she was tottering.'

Barney did not miss the exchange of glances between the two policemen.

'I didn't know all that,' Muller remarked.

'And then there was the reunion itself,' Barney continued, gaining confidence. 'You can guess how emotional it was. She'd start to cry and then she'd catch herself. And when we got up from the table, she wasn't steady on her feet and her breath seemed to come in gasps. Of course I noticed. But was that unusual under the circumstances? We all tried persuading her to take a nap. She was the one who insisted on going to the Sloan. Paul did everything except carry her to bed, but even he wasn't thinking in terms of a doctor.'

The mildness of Captain Muller's voice should have been warning enough. 'That's very clear, and I'm glad to have your description of the party. But you've left a lot out, haven't you? The way I hear it, most of the people there wanted to take control of the company away from Paul Parajian, and this little lady, alive, was going to stop them. But the minute she was dead, their position would be stronger than ever.'

Barney did not reply directly. 'Somebody's been talking,' he said darkly, before giving a bitter laugh. 'But God, that shouldn't surprise me. Everything around here is public property.'

Captain Muller liked to give his witnesses enough time to absorb the full weakness of their position. 'You can see how that leaves a lot of questions to be answered,' he said gently. 'For starters, did you know about Mrs Aratounian's will?'

'Sure I did. Harriet told me all about it. She was glad and so was I.' Barney fidgeted uncomfortably. 'We figured it would be a big help. The Aratounian trust is big money by now. Nobody was going to risk offending the old lady if it meant kissing good-bye to that inheritance.'

'Someone seems to have found a way around the problem,' the Captain pointed out. 'When you say they wouldn't risk offending her, you mean by challenging her identity, don't you?'

Unhappily, Barney nodded.

'Well, did they? Or did they all go along with the game of good old Aunt Veron?'

'They'd agreed not to raise the issue on her first day. That was after Paul told them about the will. So you see, it was already doing some good.'

'Never mind what they agreed to. What did they actually do?' Captain Muller had put his finger on the evasion.

For the first time Barney Olender relaxed. 'Don't ask me,' he said defiantly. 'They were all talking Armenian and I don't understand a word. I spent most of my time with Khassim.'

It was an obstacle the police had not expected. 'But they didn't leave you totally out of it – not if you were sitting at the same table,' Muller persisted. 'You must have had some idea of what was going on.'

Having found his foxhole, Barney Olender had no intention of abandoning it. 'Almost none,' he said shortly. 'Oh, Paul translated the toast when we drank, something about welcoming the new arrival under the roof. And I heard Alex say that Veron was very anxious to know how many children everybody had – but nothing more than that.'

'Great,' said Muller who was looking sourer and sourer. 'And I suppose you don't know anything about access to nitrites. You don't even know what they are, no matter what language you use.'

Given Barney's past performance, Muller had expected another blanket disclaimer. He was surprised to see Olender give a convulsive start.

'Nitrites?' Barney asked, stalling desperately. 'What kind?'

'Any kind,' Muller shot back.

Barney smiled weakly. 'Well, there's my heart pills. I take them occasionally, and – '

But Muller was not giving him time to babble his way off target. 'Nitroglycerin, you mean? Did you have them at the party?'

'I must have. I always carry them in my breast pocket.'

'Shirt or coat?' barked Muller.

Barney was looking more and more unhappy. 'Coat,' he admitted sullenly.

Muller was leaning back, almost genial. 'Take your coat off?'

'Never! Not for one minute!' Barney sounded ready to go to the stake.

Muller appraised him. 'All right,' he said slowly. 'Have you got the pills with you now?'

Barney, who was in shirt sleeves, swiveled to check the coat rack in the corner where his jacket was hanging. 'They're over there,' he said, rising.

Muller barred the way. 'How many pills are you carrying around?'

'Oh, I don't know exactly. It must be almost a full bottle. I haven't taken one for a month or so.'

With catlike speed, Muller was in the corner and back. 'Here!' he said, thrusting the jacket at Barney. 'Let's have a look.'

Obediently Olender extracted a small phial and held it up to the light. 'You can see for yourself, if you ...' He broke off in midsentence, color draining from his face.

'Yes,' said Muller heavily, 'I can see.'

There were only three tablets remaining in the brown plastic container. Wordlessly Barney sank back into his chair while Muller spelled it out:

'There's a handful missing, Mr Olender.'

'Anybody could have taken them when I wasn't here,' Barney protested. 'I leave my jacket here all the time.'

'It's possible,' Muller admitted neutrally.

'You don't think – '

'Right now I'm not thinking anything,' Muller told him. 'But I'm going to know a lot more after I've talked to every single person who works for this outfit.'

4. The Rest is Lies

Banks rarely have to ring twice. Late the same day, the entire Parajian family converged on Harriet's living room to listen to John Thatcher. By that time, Barney Olender's revelations were common knowledge.

'The police suspect that one of us poisoned Veron with some of Barney's nitroglycerin,' said Paul Parajian after the introductions. 'We're in trouble and there's no use denying it.'

Thatcher always appreciated having his dirty work done by someone else. Certainly this bald statement made it easier for the Sloan to crack the whip. He examined the man who was providing such unexpected help. Paul Parajian was an imposing figure with a shock of gray hair topping a square, craggy head. Even sprawled in an armchair, he seemed to dominate the gathering.

'I'm glad that you have put the situation so plainly,' Thatcher replied. 'Because the police suspicions must inevitably affect the actions of the Sloan. I hope to explain that to you.'

Lois Parajian was a specialist in futile protest. 'But that's simply ridiculous. She was a very old woman, and she died. That's all there is to it. There's no reason for all this fuss.'

Naturally Thatcher had been curious to meet Gabler's *bête noire*; now he was even more curious to observe the family's reaction to her. After all, Lois had been spear-heading a rebellion endorsed by a substantial number of them. But if the next few minutes were any guide, not many Parajians wished to be associated with her current tactics.

'If the police say she was poisoned, they know what they're talking about,' Alex Daniels said curtly.

Mark Parajian, his elbows planted on his knees, had been studying the rug. Now he lifted his head to glower at his sister-in-law. 'Don't try to act as if you're above it all, Lois. We're in this together.'

Even Gregory Parajian was forced to demur. 'Now, honey, you can't expect the Sloan to just ignore the police. That wouldn't be reasonable, would it?' Sitting on the arm of his wife's chair, he leaned forward to press her hand.

Gregory was a fined-down version of his father. He had the same abundant coarse hair and dark eyes, but they accentuated a fairer complexion. When he appeared in public with his tall blond wife, they were regularly described as a striking couple. Thatcher found he could restrain his enthusiasm for both of them.

But it was Harriet Parajian who took the firmest line. 'You've left out a good deal, Lois,' she said, gently reproachful. 'It's true that Veron was old and she had suffered many losses. But this should have been a time of happiness for her. She was reunited with her family. She was looking for affection and security. And instead ...' Harriet did not finish the sentence, but the accusation rang in the air.

Paul Parajian moved behind the couch to plant his hands on his wife's shoulders. 'It's time somebody said that,' he growled. 'I know we have a hard road ahead of us and I know that we all want to protect the family, but the least we can do for Veron is bury her with decent sadness. In spite of the fact that you're all feeling impatient with old age.'

In Thatcher's opinion this was a masterful performance. Lois' chin had lifted mutinously under Harriet's rebuke, but now she was biting her lip with vexation. And the final thrust made Gregory redden with confusion and sent Mark back to his study of the rug. Certainly Paul Parajian did not look like the embodiment of old age at the moment. His stride to the couch had been vigorous and purposive. He was standing foursquare and he was giving the orders. It was hard to believe that this was the seventy-year-old man his children wanted to consign to retirement.

They would do better to listen to him. Thatcher had not overlooked that reference to protecting the family. Paul Parajian was warning his children that the enemy was the Police Department, not the Sloan Guaranty Trust. Thatcher decided to take advantage of this distinction.

'Of course, we have no interest in Mrs Aratounian's death except as it relates to the trust we manage,' he said fluently. 'But that leaves us with a good many administrative problems. We have no way at the moment of knowing who is the beneficial owner of the trust corpus. We do, however, have a duty to protect the rights of that beneficiary, whoever it may be. With respect to most of the holdings, that simply means continuing our policy of prudent investment. But when it comes to the stock in Parajians, Incorporated, we have a difficulty. That means –'

It was too much to hope that these carefully selected phrases would divert Lois Parajian for long.

'But I told Mr Gabler,' she interrupted impatiently. 'We want the stock in our names, so we can vote it.'

'You did what?' Paul Parajian's thunder made the whole room jump.

Lois was defiant. 'I don't see why you should be so surprised. After all, you were trying to get that stock voted. So I called Mr Gabler and – '

She did not get any further. Mark Parajian was as dumbfounded as his father. 'You mean you had the nerve to claim we were in on this?'

'But we were all agreed.' Lois became reasonable. 'It's only logical to take advantage of her will.'

'So damned logical you didn't breathe a word about what you were up to. From here on, leave me out of your stupid, silly little ploys!'

Gregory stirred unhappily. 'Oh, now look, Mark, maybe Lois should have talked to you, but you know she meant it for the best.'

'You don't understand, Greg.' Alex Daniels' very softness emphasized his words. 'Mark is objecting to the fact that Lois has publicly handed him a motive for murdering Veron. He doesn't like it, and neither do I. You may not mind your wife getting deeper into this mess, but I don't want her dragging Sara with her.'

'That's enough!' shouted Paul Parajian. He paused as if he were deliberately slowing the tempo of the argument. 'I was taken by surprise at what Lois has done. But it's spilt milk now. We'll have to live with it. Probably the police would have found out anyhow, even if Veron's will is in Teheran.'

Thatcher seized the opportunity that had opened before him.

'That brings me to another consideration,' he said swiftly. 'To the best of my knowledge, Mrs Aratounian's will is still a matter of hearsay. First of all, we have a question of identity to be resolved. Only then will the matter of a testamentary disposition of the stock become relevant. In the meantime, the Sloan would like to be reassured that the stock will not become critical in any decision with respect to the company. And I think you should be prepared for a fairly lengthy interval before any of these problems can be laid to rest.'

How specific would he have to get, he wondered. The comprehension in Paul Parajian's eyes told him that one member of the audience had taken his point. Veron Aratounian's stock was not going to be delivered into the hands of her murderer.

Fortunately, Lois Parajian had been too mortified to raise further objections. And Sara Daniels seemed genuinely in search of enlightenment.

'But what are we going to do? Parajians has to go on.'

Her father had the answer. 'We'll simply have to try to work things out ourselves,' he said soothingly. 'I think Mr Thatcher is telling us this is not the time to rock the boat. But I'm sure that we can come to some interim arrangement.'

There was a sudden guffaw from Mark. 'You mean you think you can talk us all around while we're waiting,' he said half-admiringly.

'We'll have to manage things on a day-to-day basis,' his father persisted.

Mark sobered. 'Not if your idea of a day-to-day basis means an expansion that will ruin the company.'

'Oh, the company's stronger than you think,' Paul shot back. 'It's survived my mistakes for over forty years.'

'Now, I didn't say that,' Mark said defensively. 'I know you built Parajians up from nothing. All I said –'

'Do you have to say it now?' asked Alex Daniels wearily.

Reminded of the presence of an outsider, Mark subsided. 'Oh, all right,' he agreed. 'We can go into that later.'

'In between police interrogations,' Paul said pleasantly. 'I assume they've made appointments with all of you.'

Gloomily everyone agreed.

'The police are busy now at the store,' Parajian explained to Thatcher. 'One of the reasons that I asked you to come here was to leave them a clear field.'

'I didn't realize that the store had anything to do with it.'

'Only indirectly. Barney Olender, who is my assistant, was here at our lunch for Veron. The police think his heart medicine was used to poison her. They've been establishing the fact that we all knew about Barney's nitroglycerin and could have helped ourselves to it.' Suddenly his eyes twinkled. 'Even Lois made one of her rare visits to Parajians last week and had the misfortune to visit Barney's room.'

'You mean they've been asking questions about me?' The affront was enough to bring her bolt upright. 'Well, I like that!'

'When you see them, you can explain how they should concentrate on the rest of us,' said Alex, helpfully.

Lois blinked. 'I didn't mean that,' she said uncertainly. 'I just meant –'

'Perhaps,' said Harriet Parajian, 'it would be better if you didn't explain what you meant.'

Sara Daniels' giggle elicited a cautionary look from her stepmother. It seemed to be Harriet's function to bring some measure of decorum to the Parajians' social conduct. If so, thought Thatcher, she had her work cut out for her.

'You realize,' he said, 'that regardless of the police activity, the Sloan's first step will necessarily be establishing Mrs Aratounian's *bona fides*.' Mindful of his duty to the absent Gabler, Thatcher did his best. 'Now that the question has been raised, we will have to make rigorous inquiries.'

'I see that. Anything you want,' Parajian said quickly, unwilling to stir up another scene.

But Gabler would never have let him off the hook that easily.

Thatcher opened a small notebook. 'We'll start with Mrs Aratounian's emergence in Teheran.'

'The man for you to see is Hector Khassim,' said Parajian. 'He can tell you much more than I can. He was there in Teheran, and fortunately, he's here in New York now. I'll tell him that you have my full authority.'

'Perhaps that would be best,' Thatcher agreed. 'I think we've done all that we can for the moment. If any problems come up concerning the management of the company, Mr Parajian, I'm sure you'll see that we're informed.'

Parajian's white teeth glinted. 'I certainly will.'

As the problem could only be a challenge to Paul Parajian's control, Thatcher knew he could rely on this assurance. But he doubted that any emergency calls for help would be forthcoming. As they made their farewells, the younger Parajians were a subdued lot. They were, after all, facing a police investigation that was likely to present graver threats than any temporary setback to their Oriental-rug business.

'Then if you'll get in touch with Mr Khassim right away,' Thatcher concluded the interview, 'he and I should be able to meet tomorrow.'

With Gabler out of town, it was safe for Thatcher to stop by his office before calling it a day. He could pick up some papers and go straight home.

Although it was well past five, Miss Corsa was still at her desk. Her excuse, an unfinished report, was plausible, but Thatcher suspected that she simply wanted to deliver her message in person.

'A Captain Muller from the Police Department called,' she informed him. 'He wants to discuss Mrs Aratounian's trust. Mrs Norris told him that Mr Gabler was away, but that you –'

'Oh, no you don't!' Thatcher was vehement. One hot potato a day was enough. 'Gabler will be back tomorrow. He can tell the police all they want to know.'

Miss Corsa reached for the phone. By the time Thatcher was shoveling the latest psychiatric profile of British financiers into his briefcase, she reported that his message had been relayed.

'Fine!' said Thatcher.

'Good night, Mr Thatcher,' she replied without a vestige of reproach.

When he caught up with her at the elevator, this circumstance was sinking in. All too frequently, Miss Corsa wanted him to measure up to her own high standards. If she was not thrusting him into the arms of Captain Muller, why had she bothered to stay late?

As they descended, Thatcher found out.

Miss Corsa, that paragon of detachment, had been aroused by the Parajians.

'The nurse said that Mrs Daniels wasn't even crying,' she said disapprovingly.

Everett Gabler had not thought to report this detail. For the first time Thatcher realized that all ranks of the Sloan had been treated to vivid descriptions of Veron Aratounian's dying moments in the lobby.

Miss Corsa had her softer side.

'I feel so sorry for the whole family,' she murmured.

Thatcher wondered how she would feel if she met Lois Parajian. But he held his tongue and was rewarded with a rare insight into life as it was lived by the numerous Corsas in Queens.

'I couldn't help thinking how terrible it would have been if it had been my Aunt Gelsemina.'

'Oh?' Thatcher encouraged.

'Of course, she isn't my aunt. She's my grandfather's sister. I think that makes her my great-aunt.'

Thatcher thought so too.

'Nobody had seen her for fifty years,' Miss Corsa explained, making it sound like two centuries. 'Until last summer.'

'Did she come to visit you, after all that time?' Thatcher asked.

'Oh, no!' Miss Corsa destroyed the parallel. 'For their golden anniversary, we gave Grandma and Grandpa two weeks in Aversa. That's not far from Naples.'

For one of the few Americans of her generation who had never visited Europe, Miss Corsa had the geography of southern Italy pat.

'And did they enjoy themselves?'

'My grandfather did.' Miss Corsa paused. 'Grandma missed her washing machine.'

Seeing that Mr Thatcher was out of his depth, she amplified: 'My grandfather said everything was just the same as it had been. He said that Aunt Gelsemina and everybody else looked even better than when he left.'

As Thatcher's own marriage had taught him, women were the only realists. 'And your grandmother?'

'She didn't recognize anybody,' Miss Corsa replied. 'And she says that Atlantic City is good enough for her.'

'Fifty years is a long time,' Thatcher observed diplomatically.

That was exactly what Miss Corsa's grandmother had said.

5. Who is the Potter?

Captain Muller did not know he was playing with fire when he asked Everett Gabler for information. Nobody on the sixth floor of the Sloan was particularly surprised, the next morning, to see him emerge from an hour-long deluge of facts and figures looking battered and exhausted.

Gabler, on the other hand, was raring to go – and to take John Thatcher with him.

'Come on, John,' he said eagerly, 'I don't want us to be late for Khassim.'

Within half an hour, they were being ushered into the room Parajians reserved for important visitors. It was more like a shah's palace than an office. Three rugs lay on the floor, each small, each a masterpiece, each perfect in its setting. But pride of place had been given to an ancient silken Kazvin that dominated the far wall. Its intricate pattern shimmered under the carefully controlled lighting, so that complex interlacings fused into a molten glow of old copper and gold and bronze.

Thatcher found himself looking across a coffee table to see his subordinate enthroned against a background worthy of the hawklike magnificence of a desert chieftain. For a moment the juxtaposition was unsettling. Then sanity asserted itself. The sheikh who originally bought that rug had been like rich men the world over. He had hired disadvantaged Bedouins to ride around the desert while he sat in his tent, getting fat and lazy.

'... and now that a question of identity has arisen, we would welcome your assistance,' Gabler was saying fussily. 'Mr Parajian is in agreement with our activities.'

Hector Khassim smiled blandly. 'But there is no longer any question, is there? I thought the family was now satisfied.'

'In the present situation, the family may not be completely

impartial.' Thatcher was willing to match smoothness with smoothness. 'The Sloan will require more objective proof of identity.'

'The present situation?' asked Khassim. 'You are referring to Mrs Aratounian's will?'

'No,' said Thatcher. 'I was referring to her murder.'

'I see.' Khassim thoughtfully examined his fingers. When he finally looked up, he seemed to have come to a decision. 'I will not deny I have been aware of the dissension about Mrs Aratounian. Last week I would have said this was a private matter. But no longer. What is it that you wish to know?'

Gabler hitched himself forward. 'Will you describe the precise nature of Mrs Aratounian's arrival in Iran?'

Khassim blinked. He had been braced for a different question. 'But there is very little to tell. She came to my office on July seventh.'

'Just like that?' Gabler pressed. 'With no advance warning? Not even a telephone call?'

'Exactly. I was sitting at my desk when my clerk came in. I can remember the details vividly. It was a shock, you understand. He said there was an elderly woman who appeared to be sick in the waiting room. She insisted on seeing me and had written her name down. I will give you the exact words she had written. Her name was in the Russian style – Veron Gregorievna Aratounian. After it she had simply written, "Paul Parajian's sister."'

'And what did you do?'

'I was electrified. I ran to the waiting room and there she was, a huddled heap in dusty clothes, very weak. I was too excited to think clearly about the orders I was giving. Soon all the clerks were rushing about – one to get a doctor, one to fetch a tray of food, another to lead her to a comfortable office.' The memory was still powerful enough to move Khassim. He took out a handkerchief and mopped his brow. 'It was all very dramatic.'

If he was hoping to spark some human sympathy, he had misread his man. Everett Gabler was rigid with censure. 'And you did all this without any attempt to verify the woman's identity?'

'Mr Gabler!' Khassim was deeply shocked. 'She was a Parajian!'

'And what if she were not?'

'I was more concerned with the consequences if she was.' Khassim shifted his bulk and spoke earnestly. 'Paul and I have been associates for almost forty years. I know how he feels about family obligations. What would you expect me to do? Let his sister faint from hunger in my presence while I investigated? What do you think he would say to me? I did what I knew he would want. I tended to Mrs Aratounian's immediate needs, and I placed an urgent call to New York.'

'Ah!'

It would be better for everyone, Thatcher thought, if Everett could refrain from sounding like a prosecutor. Hastily he inserted a neutral question.

'And was Mr Parajian surprised?'

'He was astounded. And, of course, very concerned about his sister's medical condition as soon as I described her. Immediately he insisted that I get the best doctors, specialists if necessary, that everything be done for her comfort. We were on the phone two and three times a day for that first week. The doctors advised complete rest, and she was a little difficult about that. But Paul insisted that the doctors' advice be followed. Finally she agreed to a convalescent home for a few weeks. It did her a great deal of good.'

'That is very interesting,' Thatcher commented. 'It has been suggested that Parajian was very anxious to rush his sister over here so that she could vote her stock immediately.'

Khassim emitted a rich sound of disgust. 'Those children, they will say anything. Naturally Paul realized that Veron's arrival could solve all his problems. But he was scrupulous that her health should come first. He was agreeable that she should remain in the nursing home as long as it would benefit her. And even when she came out, he would not hear of her traveling alone. My own annual trip to New York was scheduled for mid-August, and he insisted that she wait to travel with me so that I could look after her. If anything, Paul bent over backwards not to rush her.'

'I am glad to hear it,' said Gabler, reentering the fray. 'Let us hope that the woman he was so concerned for turns out to have been his sister. But, Mr Khassim, one thing still puzzles me. If you do business with the Parajians and you know the children, you must have thought you knew the entire family. Weren't you startled when an unknown sister suddenly appeared on the scene?'

'Mr Gabler, I have always known about Veron.' Khassim was indulgent. 'I first met Paul when he was working for a cheap rug factory in Greece. They used to send him to Iran to find designs they could copy. In a very real sense, I am his permanent office in Iran. That is why Veron came to me.'

Opponents often thought they had scored a victory over Gabler. Thatcher recognized the silence for what it was: Everett was catching his breath for the next round.

'The Parajians were fortunate to have an old family friend on the scene,' Thatcher said, marking time. 'We didn't realize that your association with them was virtually lifelong.'

Khassim enjoyed basking in the reflected glory of the Parajian empire. 'Paul has traveled a long road. When I first knew him, he looked half starved, the way all the Armenians did. Of course, with his whole family depending on him, he was afraid all the time – afraid of not satisfying his employers, then later afraid his business would fail. But what a difference after the war! By 1950, he was a man of substance. He was confident, assured. He had a delightful second wife, his hair was gray, he had put on weight.' Khassim looked down at his own *embonpoint* complacently. 'But I too have changed. It is wonderful what differences success can accomplish.'

Unwittingly, Khassim had challenged his guests to visualize him forty years ago. The picture was irresistible. He would have been thin, restless, ill at ease. The hard part was connecting that boy with this balding man of affairs. If Paul Parajian had gone up like a meteor, Hector Khassim had shared the ascent.

'You have reminded us how people change over the course of time,' Gabler said. 'Presumably that applies to Mrs Aratounian too.'

'Of course it does,' Khassim agreed. 'The only time I met her in the old days, she was a young bride.'

Gabler shifted his ground. 'Did you see much of her in Iran?'

There was a touch of rebuke in Khassim's reply. 'Naturally I made it a point to do so. I visited her regularly in the nursing home. Then, when we agreed that she should wait until my flight, I moved her to my own home for the last week. I even summoned my granddaughter to be her companion. There were many little errands where she needed help – shopping and that sort of thing.'

These were not the details Gabler wanted. 'Did she speak much about the past? Did she describe her trip from Russia, or did she recall her childhood with her brother?'

'I see what you have in mind.' Khassim cocked his head alertly. 'But I do not think she said much that would be helpful to you. When she was in the nursing home, I told her about my phone calls with Paul. She was anxious to hear as much about him as possible. They had been very close as children. Then when she was staying with me, she spoke to Paul directly. That was when he warned her about the trouble with the children, and when she decided to make her will.'

Gabler could recognize a red herring, but this one was too attractive to dismiss.

'What was her attitude toward the quarrel?' he asked. 'Was it your impression that she would have sided with her brother?'

'Of that there can be no doubt.' Khassim decided to expand. 'She was contemptuous about the children. She said they reminded her of her brother Haig, always pretending he knew better than his big brother. It stood to reason that since Paul had built up the business, he should run it. She was an old-fashioned woman, with respect for the head of the family.' Khassim sighed deeply. 'In many ways, family life was easier in those days.'

That red herring Everett could ignore with ease. 'Now, Mr Khassim,' he said implacably, 'I understand why you could not cross-examine a sick woman in a nursing home. But you had over a month to make inquiries. What did you do?'

'Nothing.' Khassim spread his hands in the age-old gesture. 'I had informed Paul of all the circumstances. He did not ask me to take any action. And after all, why should he? The Parajian family is not international news. How many people knew of Paul's sister in Soviet Armenia? You are thinking of an imposture now only because the children raised the question. But they were acting out of self-interest. If Mrs Aratounian had not owned any stock, it would never have occurred to them to question her identity.'

Thatcher was happy to see Gabler bite back the obvious retort. If Mrs Aratounian had not been a rich woman, there would have been no point to any impersonation. Or to a murder. Everett simply continued digging.

'It may have been reasonable to accept this woman as Mrs Veron Aratounian,' he said with a generous air of concession. 'I merely wish to establish that she was accepted and flown off to America without any verification.'

Khassim was annoyed. 'Flying off to America from Iran is not quite that simple. I saw her passport and I thanked God for it. If the passport had not been in order, I would have had the same trouble I had with the children. They, after all, were accepted as Parajians without all this verification of which you speak.' He ended on the note of a debater making a complete and final rebuttal.

'Children?' asked Gabler blankly. 'I don't know what you're talking about.'

It was Khassim's turn to bite back an answer. Nevertheless, his face said it for him. 'What do you know?' he was asking. Ostentatiously patient, he began explaining.

'Paul's first wife died before he came to America. He couldn't bring the children, so he left them with his mother. Then war broke out. Greece was invaded, Paul's mother died, the children disappeared. It took years to locate them. We had the Red Cross and the United Nations people and the DP personnel all searching for them. It was 1948 before they were located. And I can assure you there was no nonsense about identification papers. They barely had clothes on their bodies. But when I cabled

Paul, he was jubilant. He did not raise all these difficulties that you do.'

For all practical purposes, he was accusing Gabler of being an unnatural parent.

'I recognize that a distraught father would be overjoyed to recover his lost children,' Everett said stiffly. 'The circumstances in the two cases are entirely different. Nevertheless, the background of the Parajian children comes as a surprise. I had assumed they were raised here in America.'

'That was Harriet's doing.' Khassim smiled slightly. 'Not every young woman would welcome three strange children into her home. But she never hesitated for a second. Let the three of them come at once, she said. It did not matter that they spoke no English, that they had been living like animals for years. She would take care of all that. And she did.'

'Very commendable,' began Everett. But he was destined to learn more about the Parajians.

'In the end it was just as well,' Khassim mused. 'Harriet did not have a child of her own for years. I think she would have minded a great deal if she had not had Paul's children to mother.'

'She's getting a strange return for her affection,' Thatcher said, determined to keep the conversation on the tracks.

Khassim was grimly amused. 'Mark and Gregory would tell you that they're doing it for Harriet's sake as much as their own. They're protecting her and her son from Paul's incompetence.' He laughed outright. 'They are frightened by big numbers, that is the truth of it. They have not inherited Paul's instinct for trading.'

It was a subject about which Thatcher and Gabler knew more than Hector Khassim, and they were unable to display any real astonishment. But undeterred, Khassim continued to expatiate on the topic until the end of their visit.

'Well,' said Thatcher once they were back on Fifth Avenue, 'he gave us more than one pointer, didn't he?'

Everett's nod was perfunctory. 'Yes. John, did you notice the significant part of his story about Mrs Aratounian?'

Thatcher did not break stride. 'I could scarcely have missed it. Khassim told us that no outsider could have known enough about the Parajians to bring in a fake Mrs Aratounian. But at the same time he revealed that he himself knew everything relevant.'

'And,' said Everett pounding in the final nail, 'he had all the time in the world to coach an impostor.'

'So that she could play her role – for as long as was necessary.'

The contempt that Hector Khassim expressed for Paul Parajian's children was genuine enough. But he was not above taking out insurance. That evening found him playing host as the sommelier hovered with a heroic wine list.

'I am so happy that you could join me for dinner,' he said, seating Lois Parajian with elaborate care. 'As I told you, Gregory, we have important matters to discuss ...'

6. Gently, Brother, Gently

Every family needs a peacemaker – particularly when the family includes several households all drawing financially from the same well. Harriet Parajian had been playing this role for many years. It was only an extension of her earlier activities – composing the childhood quarrels of Gregory and Sara or mediating between Paul and a teen-aged Mark. If asked, the Parajians would have agreed that Harriet had no axe to grind, Harriet could be trusted, Harriet was simply interested in family harmony. All this was perfectly true. But Harriet knew in her bones what a lot of men sitting around conference tables learn the hard way: peace-making always involved policy decisions.

By the next morning she had decided on her strategy.

Sara Daniels answered the phone at the first ring.

'Oh, Harriet,' she said, disappointed, 'I was hoping it would be the man at Macy's.'

Harriet never took offense where none was intended. Two years ago Alex Daniels had been the victim of a personnel cutback at his electronics company. The Danielses had then sold their suburban condominium, moved forty miles upstate and gone into business manufacturing a line of small, electrically heated greenhouses. Their affairs were still in a precarious condition, but the first ray of a golden dawn had appeared when the buyer for Macy's indicated a guarded interest. It was safe to say that Harriet was the only relative following every aspect of this small but tortuous saga.

'If you're expecting to hear from him, then you won't want to come into New York today,' she said, altering her plans without hesitation. 'But I do want to talk with you, Sara. How would it be if we met for lunch at the Amos Gardiner House?'

The Amos Gardiner House was two miles from the Danielses' home and thirty-eight miles from New York. Sara was no fool. A seventy-six-mile drive told its own story.

'Of course,' she said. 'Could we make it twelve thirty? Nothing will happen here between twelve and two.'

But when Sara arrived in the cool shadowed dining room, the suspense was already over.

'He called,' she announced grimly. 'He's sorry, but he has to think about it some more. Our prices aren't competitive with some outfit on the Coast.'

Even as she sympathized, Harriet cursed inwardly. She wanted Sara's undivided attention. She had not come this far to attend a wake for Green Thumbs, Unlimited.

Sara might have been a mind reader. 'Don't worry,' she said, reviving under the impact of a tall glass of iced tea. 'Alex and I both know that the worse things are with the greenhouses, the more important Parajians is to us.'

'It's not just the business,' Harriet said calmly.

'You don't have to remind me. The police were here first thing this morning.'

'I'm sure you and Alex were very sensible. But there's no use beating around the bush. Lois is likely to say anything that comes into her head, and –'

'And what?' asked Sara, puzzled. It was so well established in family lore that Lois was the menace on every conceivable occasion, she could not imagine additional bogeys.

Harriet sighed. 'I'm afraid that Hector is capable of thinking too much about his own self-interest.'

'He always has been,' said Sara shortly. 'But I honestly don't see what difference that makes now. Aunt Veron's death isn't any of his business.'

'Hector makes most of his money from Parajians. He thinks everything connected with it is his business.'

'Yes, but –'

Firmly Harriet swept on. 'And we have to be realistic. I don't know how, but in some way Veron's death was connected with her stock in Parajians. The police are going on that assumption, and we'd be fools not to.'

'But Daddy didn't say anything about this the other day,' Sara protested.

'Paul has his hands full trying to keep Lois from incriminating everyone in the family,' Harriet said tartly. 'She is drawing quite enough attention to us. Sara, I want you to talk to the boys and make sure they realize this is no time to have a big fight with Paul in the office. It's not just hiding dirty linen from the Sloan. If they start one of their shouting matches, the police will know about it in ten minutes.'

She had struck the right chord.

'Good Lord, yes. I never dreamed the police could find out so much. Do you know that Captain Muller knew exactly when Alex and I had been to the office last? And he knew that I'd been in Barney's room, too. He seemed to think I should remember whether Barney's jacket was hanging on the coat rack.'

Swiftly Harriet capitalized on her advantage. 'Exactly. And you know what it's like when Paul and Mark start yelling at each other. They can be heard at the other end of the building. You have to persuade the boys to behave.'

'Well, I'm willing to give it a try,' Sara agreed dubiously. 'But I don't know how far I'll get. Mark is frightened to death of this buying trip Daddy is sending him on. He says it will lose lots of money. And Lois is dead set against it too, mostly because it was Daddy's idea.'

'Never mind how Lois feels. Concentrate on what Gregory thinks. He's your real hope.'

Sara's eyes widened. 'But Gregory always does what Lois wants. We all know that.' She began to enumerate. 'Greg would like a house up in Westchester, but they're all crammed into that apartment because Lois won't leave the city. Greg would like to spend his vacation in Amagansett with the rest of us, but they go to that dreary resort in Canada that Lois' parents discovered. For heaven's sake, Greg's even become an Episcopalian!'

'Yes, yes, I know all about that,' Harriet said impatiently. 'But none of those things are important to him. Surely you've noticed that when Gregory really cares about something, he gets his own way.'

'Such as?' challenged Sara.

'Have you forgotten that barely six months after they were married, Lois decided that he should leave Parajians and go into her uncle's firm in Philadelphia? And what about her bright idea that Barney should take over the wholesaling, so that Gregory wouldn't have to go on business trips any more?'

'And the rug,' Sara suddenly chimed in gleefully. 'I had forgotten the rya rug!'

Harriet could not help smiling. Lois' most public marital defeat had occurred when rya rugs first came into fashion. Without bothering to consult her husband, she had rushed out to become a trend setter. Gregory had returned from Texas, taken one look at his living-room floor and exploded. The shock wave reached as far as the Parajian showroom. Legend had it that Gregory took Lois by the scruff of the neck in one hand, the offending Danish import in the other, and marched them both right back to Lord & Taylor. This was probably too good to be true. But it was undeniable that the original Shiraz was down again within hours. It was still there.

'All right,' Sara conceded. 'I grant you that Greg can be pushed just so far. But he's as eager to have Daddy retire as everyone else, Harriet.'

'We're talking about the buying trip. That's the immediate problem. Mark and Lois make so much noise, it's easy to miss the fact that Gregory isn't joining in. But I think you'll find he isn't against the trip.'

Sara welcomed any reading of the situation that would make her task easier. 'If that's true, Greg can help me persuade Mark to lie low for the time being. It'll be a different kettle of fish when the Sloan releases Veron's fifteen percent.'

'Then you'll all gang up to get rid of Paul.' Harriet looked at her stepdaughter curiously. 'Has it occurred to you, Sara, when that day comes you're going to split in three separate directions, because you don't all want the same things. You and Alex, for instance – '

'Yes, yes,' Sara broke in, flushing. 'You don't have to say it. But Alex and I don't want more income for ourselves. We don't want to spend it on riotous living, or anything. It's just that if we had bigger dividends for the next three or four years, while we're getting Green Thumbs off the ground, it would make all the difference.'

'What difference? You're not in real financial danger, and you know it.'

Sara was unhappily twisting her napkin. 'I hate it when Alex has to ask Daddy for money,' she finally blurted.

'Alex seems to bear up,' Harriet observed. She always encouraged her husband to help the Danielses, but there were limits to her good nature. 'I don't think avoiding embarrassment justifies what you're doing to your father.'

'Maybe not. But Mark wants bigger dividends too.'

'Mark is simply cautious by nature. He's afraid of Paul's plans for expansion, and he's managed to convince you that more conservative management will increase the profits. I'm not at all sure that he's right about that. Anyway, I doubt if he'll ever get the chance to find out.'

Sara was taken aback. 'Why not? Sooner or later, we'll get that fifteen percent.'

'If you ever listened to a word Lois said, you'd realize what she's after. She thinks that once Paul retires, the natural thing would be to sell out.'

'Sell Parajians?' After a moment of stupefied silence, Sara's chin tightened. 'She must be crazy! I'll go along with what you said earlier. Gregory would never stand for it.'

'Ah, Gregory ...' Harriet murmured carefully. 'No, he wouldn't stand for it. Because he wants to run the business himself. And I don't think he has any intention of being conservative.'

Sara had trouble adjusting to the new vistas Harriet was opening. 'I don't understand all this,' she said slowly, 'but I think maybe I'd better go into town today after all.'

'I thought you were too busy with greenhouses to drop by anymore,' Greg greeted her.

'We're not getting much work done today. Alex and I had the police on our necks this morning.'

'We had them too. They've got this cockeyed idea we had something to gain by Veron's death.'

'Well, we all know where they got that cockeyed idea,' Sara retorted.

Mark looked up from his desk wearily. He knew that Sara and Gregory were fond of each other. He also knew that the habit of mockery can get out of hand. Sara had greenhouses that Macy's wasn't buying. Gregory had Lois. They could both draw plenty of blood. It was time to call them off.

'We've all got problems now,' he reminded them. 'The thing to do is let the police get on with their work while we get on with ours.'

Sara was quick to see an opening. 'I don't think we can treat Veron's murder that way.'

Her brothers were dismayed, more by her words than by her meaning. They had fallen into the habit of referring to their aunt's death in neutral phrases suggesting she had been a traffic fatality.

'How can you say that?' Gregory asked nervously. 'We didn't have anything to do with it.'

'Oh, Gregory. You always want to stick your head in the sand.'

'Now, wait a minute.' Mark was striving for a reassuring tone. 'Of course, I can see how it looks to outsiders. We didn't like Aunt Veron turning up when she did. Let's face it. It was damned inconvenient, and we thought it might be rigged. Then, after she was dead, it turned out we inherited her holdings. So the police are suspicious. But we know we didn't kill her.'

'You're forgetting one thing, Mark. Someone did kill her. That's what I mean about sticking your head in the sand. Alex says – '

At this familiar refrain, both her brothers snorted.

'Sure, Alex knows everything,' growled Mark.

'What makes him such an expert?' Gregory demanded.

'If you'd just listen!' Sara snapped. 'The police have proved that Veron was poisoned at our lunch. What's more, they've proved it was done with Barney's pills. That means someone in that room did it. We have to face facts.'

Her brothers looked at her, then at each other.

'All right,' said Mark cautiously. 'But where does that get us?

I still say none of us did it. And I'm not playing guessing games about anyone else who was there.'

Gregory breathed a soft sigh of relief. He was never sure in these conversations whether Lois counted as a member of the family or not. And this time, he did not want to find out.

'It means we can't run around pretending that Parajians isn't under a spotlight,' Sara insisted. 'And we've got to remember that there's a murderer who may be counting on us to do something. You may as well know that Harriet came up to have lunch with me.'

Both men relaxed. They were far more willing to have Harriet's words of wisdom repeated than Alex's.

'What did she say?' asked Mark.

'She's worried. She's afraid we may do something that looks suspicious to the police. She wants us to cool it for the time being. And that means no fight about Mark's buying trip to the Middle East.'

Mark groaned. 'I should have known. Do you realize how much money we can lose on Paul's big ideas?'

Sara waited, anxious to see if Gregory would confirm Harriet's views. But he managed to remain ambiguous.

'I don't think we should worry about that now, Mark. Sara and Harriet are right. This is no time to have a lot of gossip about a big fight at Parajians.'

Mark was still unconvinced. 'You sound pretty high-and-mighty about it, Sara. But Alex is always the first one to howl for bigger dividends.'

Sara ignored the remark. 'And there's another thing. Harriet says Daddy has his work cut out for him, trying to protect the family. He doesn't have time for management squabbles.'

'He's not the only one,' muttered Greg. 'But I see her point. The Sloan has stymied us on the main question, anyway. We're just marking time. Probably the sensible thing is to let Paul carry the ball, and support him.' He grinned crookedly at his brother and sister. 'One for all, and all for one. That's been our theme song before.'

'Yes, we need to stand together more than ever,' Sara said swiftly. 'You see that, don't you, Mark?'

Mark's filial feelings were stirred. 'It's not just a matter of sense. I agree we should stand behind Paul. We're his children, after all.' He stared almost defiantly at the others. 'Well, aren't we?'

7. A Distant Drum

Man may be able to live by bread alone, but a little bit of romance never hurts, and merchants have known this since Rome was young. Barring a prohibition by the Food and Drug Administration or the Underwriters Association, retailers will always apply some sugar coating.

And if the price is steep enough, they do not stop with a touch of illusion. They produce a full-blown melodrama. Every diamond over five carats has been owned by Marie Antoinette, Catherine the Great or both. Every aging silver bowl with more than one dent was crafted by Paul Revere.

And *all* Oriental rugs are woven by nomads pitching their tents under starry skies as they follow the seasons and the tinkling of camel bells. Very little is heard of state-supported factories and capital investments by big-city promoters.

Parajians Inc. was more discreet about the Garden of Allah than some of its competitors, but it knew exactly what its customers wanted to hear. Accordingly, its literature was strong on ancient Persia, home of the sumptuous carpet since the days of Shah Ismail.

But by the time Mark Parajian was a week into his buying trip, he was in no doubt that he was operating in the capital of modern, petroleum-exporting, Iran.

'My God, they're raising the minimum wage again,' he grumbled. 'Do they know what this is going to do to rug prices?'

Hector Khassim nodded impassively. 'They know.'

They could scarcely help knowing. Any Oriental rug is made with hand-tied knots. And quite a small size, say a five-by-seven, may well contain two and a half million such knots, each tied by nimble human fingers. Raise the pay for those fingers and a remarkable price boost is inevitable.

'And now this new child-labor law,' said Mark, who had gone on to the next government directive awaiting his attention in Khassim's office.

'The cost of progress,' Khassim told him fatalistically.

'Progress is going to drive Iran right out of the rug business,' said Mark sourly.

Any summary of recent Iranian history was bound to spell bad news for a rug buyer. First, the sons and grandsons of weavers left the loom to work in the oil fields. Then, with oil revenues piling up, the Shah decided to encourage industrial growth – and women flocked into new, better-paying occupations. Now, a new school system was going to drain the pool of weavers even more.

'The last wage increase,' Khassim mused, 'was supposed to induce the women to stay at the looms. I know the minister was surprised when it didn't work that way.'

Administrators are frequently handicapped by a lack of personal experience. The minister had never tried sitting hunched over a loom, tying eight hundred knots an hour. More than one woman could have told him – and Khassim too – that after rug-making, assembly work in a modern factory was a picnic. The blue-collar blues did not originate in Detroit with Henry Ford.

Mark Parajian had only limited interest in Iran. 'What it all boils down to is that the whole rug picture is going haywire.'

Nodding, Khassim said, 'It is indeed. But of course Paul knows this very well. On his own – and through the information I have sent him – he has kept fully informed about local conditions here.'

Mark bit back hard, but the glint in his eye was more than enough to encourage Khassim to continue: 'Although I wonder what he will say about some of the prices you have been forced to pay in the past few days.'

'He's happy,' said Mark shortly. 'Listen, I've got an appointment with Nuveri in half an hour –'

'Then it will be much quicker if we have Joseph drive us,' Khassim interjected smoothly. 'Not many taxis know the way out there.'

Khassim's methods were always unobtrusive. Now he had

learned that Mark was reporting nightly to New York. Soon, he would sit in on the negotiations with Nuveri. This was not enough to satisfy his insatiable curiosity, but it was a start.

Undeniably, however, Joseph and the resplendent Cadillac were a help – even downtown, where cranes and construction crews throttled already clogged streets. On every corner, a towering office building was going up; in between, a hotel or condominium. But Joseph came into his own when he finally left the din of building and rebuilding, and began threading his way south, through a depressing shantytown of steaming squalor. Here alleys barely wide enough for the Cadillac snaked bewilderingly, narrowed by dusty pedestrians, overburdened donkeys, scavenging dogs. Here, poverty, disease and ignorance still held undisputed, unpicturesque sway.

Avram Nuveri was not poor. Although his warehouse had an unprepossessing, shabby exterior, there were armed guards twenty-four hours a day. His Swiss doctor assured him that his health remained excellent. No one had ever had any doubts about his wits.

'*Enchanté*, *messieurs*, *enchanté*,' he said effusively. The Sorbonne figured heavily in Nuveri's happiest reminiscences, and copies of *Le Monde* and *Figaro* were strewn around like rose petals. But even during his *jeunesse doré* in Paris, Avram Nuveri had known all about the charm of drafts on the Sloan Guaranty Trust.

'... ah, of course,' he capitulated when Mark projected impatience with the ornate preliminaries. 'To business, to business. First, let me show you what we have from our own factory ...'

'I'm pretty well loaded up with junk,' said Mark indifferently. Nuveri sucked in his breath, while Khassim assumed his bloodhound expression. 'I'm interested in anything better you've got.'

'... some very fine Konyas, of an excellent weave,' said Nuveri, quivering with indignation.

Mark raised a shoulder skeptically, but studied what was spread before him. These modern rugs had been produced in village workshops owned by the Nuveris for three generations.

This interchange was as stylized as the patterns Mark was examining.

At issue were modern rugs. Some were very fine; some were total abortions. They could be sold in New York for several hundred, or several thousand dollars – with misrepresentation and downright fraud lurking in every increment. Mark Parajian had one of the sharpest eyes in the trade for this no-man's-land. At twenty yards, he could spot wool insufficiently washed, chemical dyes, false Turkish knots. But, since Parajians was a wholesaler as well as a retailer, Mark also knew how much even bad rugs can command. So he bought selectively, after ramming every defect down the seller's throat in the best tradition of bazaar haggling. Khassim had watched him pay a good price for rugs that would never see the interior of a Parajian showroom.

Avram Nuveri's new Kirmans were perfectly respectable. If the colors lacked splendor, they were eminently suited to the American preference for softer, milder hues – as, indeed, Nuveri had intended them to be.

'And some very useful sizes,' he observed, complacently ignoring Mark's bored distaste.

No inspection by Mark Parajian was ever perfunctory. It took over an hour for ten rugs to change hands.

'But I believe your father is interested in some antiques,' said Nuveri slyly, as if Mark's activities had not been the talk of Teheran for days. 'How wise he is! What better investment now? Let me show you . . .'

It was salt in an open wound. The rich of Iran, including Avram Nuveri, had been hoarding rugs as an inflation hedge – classic antiques when they could get them, otherwise the cream of recent production. And now, Paul Parajian had sent his oldest son over with a blank check and orders to buy, buy, buy.

Mark Parajian had been buying every treasure he could find. He was still doing so, and when they left, Nuveri was rubbing his hands as contentedly as if he had never had the benefits of a French education.

'It is always a pleasure to do business with Parajians,' he said.

'Send my respectful regards to your father – and also my profound condolences. Death is sorrowful enough without a gathering of the vultures ...'

It took all of Hector Khassim's diplomatic skill to extricate Mark before he exploded.

'What the hell was that old thief talking about?'

Fortunately, they were safely back in the Cadillac when the question erupted.

Folding his hands over his paunch, Khassim tested the ground. 'Thief? No doubt, Nuveri's prices have risen. Still, I do not think you will regret – '

'I regret it right now,' Mark snapped back. 'What I want to know is what that crack about vultures meant.'

'I assume Nuveri was alluding – delicately – to the tax collectors,' said Khassim. 'That, of course, is the usual conclusion when inquiries are made in Iran.'

He cocked an eye. Mark looked baffled, so Khassim decided to twist the knife a little. 'Did you think that the authorities would forget that Veron was murdered?'

Outside, the battle of horns continued with ear-splitting monotony. Joseph, alternating short bursts of speed with sudden, screeching swerves, was making slow progress back toward Khassim's office on Pahlevi Square. Khassim was not displeased to have this interlude.

'Do you mean to tell me' – Mark was thunderstruck – 'that the police have been asking questions over here?'

'I do not know about the police,' said Khassim, lying fluently. His cousin in the Ministry of Justice kept him up to date. 'But the Sloan Guaranty Trust has stirred up a hornet's nest. As Nuveri shows, nothing can be kept secret in Teheran for long. My banker tells me that there are new questions about me in every mail – my movements, my credit rating, my connections with the Soviet Union. It is only reasonable to assume that other investigations are under way as well.'

The bewilderment on Mark's face sharpened Khassim's voice. 'Do you think that a large bank like the Sloan simply accepts the fact that Mrs Aratounian first appeared here in Teheran? No, of course not. At this very moment, I am sure they are making overtures to the Soviet Union, to be sure that Paul's sister is not still alive and well – in Yerevan!'

Mark was not worrying about Soviet Armenia. 'Why you?' he asked nervously. 'You didn't vouch for her or anything.'

Khassim smiled blandly. 'The Sloan may be suspicious of the number of Parajians who have commenced prosperous existence under my auspices. When they learned that I, in effect, sponsored you – and Sara and Gregory too, of course – they immediately began investigating my banking arrangements with the United States for the past twenty-five years – '

'Wait!' Mark held both hands to his head as if he could not believe what he was hearing. 'Hold it right there! What about your banking arrangements in the past twenty-five years? What do they expect to discover from them?'

'They want to be sure I am not being paid off.'

'By whom?'

Khassim sighed. 'By you.'

While Mark stared, Khassim drove the point home. 'The possibility of Veron's imposture, you see, has opened a Pandora's box.'

'You mean they think I'm not Mark Parajian?' Mark asked dully. 'They're out of their minds. I haven't spent my life behind the Iron Curtain, like Veron. I've been in the front office of Parajians for everybody to see – '

'Perhaps it is the period before you went to work at Parajians that interests them,' said Khassim.

'Jesus Christ! I wasn't a baby in 1948. I was seventeen years old when I went to live with my father. A man recognizes his own son, doesn't he?'

'Of course we know this is nonsense, Mark,' said Khassim soothingly. 'But try to see the other point of view. Paul had not seen you since you were four. And let us be honest about it. Can you pretend that when you were reunited, you regaled him with memories of your childhood?'

Mark was sticking with his own point of view. 'I was in no shape to swap stories with anybody,' he said gruffly. 'I was wrapped in a cocoon of concrete!'

But Khassim was a masterful devil's advocate. 'I know, I know. After all, it was through hospital records that I located you. But consider how this looks to the Sloan. A young laborer is seriously injured in a construction accident. He proves to be Mark Parajian, who leads the way to the refugee camp where Sara and Gregory are. They are too young for memories. How unfortunate that the oldest child should be too weak to talk to his father . . .'

'As a matter of fact, I didn't see that much of Paul when I first got to New York,' Mark said, softening slightly. 'Harriet was the one who came to the hospital every day. She spent hours with me. By the time I threw my crutches away, she had me talking English – '

'And looking to the future,' Khassim contributed. 'When you rejoined the family, the past was dead. Gregory and Sara were American schoolchildren. You were ready to go to work. Nobody wanted to talk about Greece or the war – '

'We wanted to forget it,' Mark insisted.

'Very natural – and very convenient!'

'Convenient, hell!' said Mark angrily. 'Besides, how does a man prove he's himself? Particularly if he's been mixed up in a war. I was in a displaced-persons camp like lots of other people. Say, that's how to do it! There must be plenty of people who were with me, who know who I am.'

Deliberately, Khassim contradicted him. 'No, Mark. There were people who shared a barracks with you. Some of them have seen you since. But how could they recognize the starved scrap of humanity they had known? When Paul brought you over on your first buying trip, you had become another rich American. They accepted you at your own valuation, and said wasn't it wonderful what luck could do.'

By now Mark was tired of the subject. 'All right,' he said defiantly. 'I say I'm Mark Parajian. Paul says I'm Mark Parajian – '

'And I know that you are Mark Parajian,' Khassim interjected. Like Mark, he was ready to end this small incursion into the past. Reminders are useful only if they point the way to the future. 'Oh, here we are. Will you come in for a drink?'

Mark had already dined twice in Hector's spacious villa, silhouetted against the snow-capped Elburz Mountains. 'I think I'll get back to the hotel,' he said. 'There are some calls I've got to make. Then I want to pack. I'm making an early start tomorrow.'

'You're sure you will not reconsider, and take Joseph and the car?' asked Khassim.

'Absolutely,' said Mark, with more firmness than courtesy. The helicopter to Ispahan was not a prospect that appealed, but he wanted to leave Hector Khassim behind.

'Then at least, we will take you to the airport,' said Khassim, in tones that brooked no refusal. 'I shall join you for breakfast.'

Hector Khassim had more to say, and if Mark Parajian had not been so preoccupied, he would have realized it.

As it was, he was caught unaware the following morning. Over breakfast at the Teheran Hilton, Khassim chatted knowledgeably and helpfully about the Bakhtiari weavers that Mark was planning to visit in the south. With timing that was not coincidental, Joseph was stowing Mark's suitcase into the car when Khassim made his first pass at the subject.

'And did you speak to Paul last night about your purchases from Nuveri?'

'I did,' said Mark repressively.

'And was he pleased?'

'He still thinks he's grabbing a golden opportunity,' Mark replied, stooping to climb into the back seat.

Keeping in the good graces of both father and son, even while they were locked in a festering dispute, posed only minor problems for anyone as astute as Hector Khassim. But it was the future of Parajians that exercised him. So he chose his words with care

'Paul is taking a great chance,' he said sympathetically. 'I understand why you are concerned. But Mark, have you thought past that? What if Paul is correct, as he has so often been in the past? He will make an enormous amount of money.'

Mark's grunt was ambiguous, but enough to hearten Khassim. Dinner with Mr and Mrs Gregory Parajian had not been reassuring. Lois' plans for the future did not include rug stores or Hector Khassim. As usual, Gregory had let his wife do the talking. Mark's commitment seemed more promising.

'When I was in New York,' Khassim said, almost apologetically, 'the course of events prevented my talking in any great detail with Paul. But, from our few words, I gathered he was still interested ...'

'Interested in what?' Mark asked with quick suspicion.

'Why, this idea about India and Pakistan,' said Khassim, careful not to name a source. 'As you yourself have said, the rug situation in this part of the world is in flux. What better idea than a partnership with some government-sponsored looms in India and Pakistan – where they do not have oil money pouring in. Surely Paul has mentioned this to you.'

'I've more or less stopped listening to these grandiose plans Paul keeps having,' Mark said. Then, involuntarily, he gave these words the lie. 'It's the craziest thing I've ever heard of. How could it work? We'd be getting in over our heads – government training, subsidies, tax deals. We're sellers – not producers!'

They had arrived at the airport and Mark's hand was on the door.

'Some of the great rug fortunes have been made that way – '

'This isn't the time for it,' Mark interrupted. 'Look, I've got to get going. I'll check back with you before I leave for Tabriz. In the meantime, try lining up some shipping space.'

When his last-minute instructions were over, Mark strode through the crowd, with Joseph scurrying after him.

Khassim watched until they were out of sight, then sat back to wait. For all this show of decision, he thought, Mark Parajian was a timid man. Any bold plan was beyond his ingrained caution.

'To the office, Joseph,' he ordered when his driver returned.

Joseph heard the undertone and outdid himself trying to beat every other car on the road.

But the exasperated drumming of Khassim's fingers was not directed at his chauffeur, but at fate.

Paul Parajian had been timid and cautious too when he set

off for America. But time had transformed him into a man of self-confidence and vision. And Hector Khassim had shared only a fraction of this brilliant success.

Now another brilliant success lay within reach. This time, Hector Khassim intended to share in it fully. But there were obstacles, among them timid, fearful Mark ...

'There must be a way,' he said, unconscious of having spoken aloud. 'There must be a way ...'

By the time he got back to his own office, his fertile brain had suggested not one, but several.

8. Some Buried Caesar

Paul Parajian was pleased with the reports Mark was telephoning regularly from Teheran, Tabriz and Ispahan. But his determination to stage the most magnificent sale of his career did not rest with sending his elder son to the fabled Middle East. Since he was resolved to offer treasures from the four corners of the earth, he had to go nearer.

So, while Mark scoured Nain and Qum, Gregory headed for Lansing, Michigan, where Rear Admiral Homer Christiansen, USN (Ret.), was a tougher proposition than Avram Nuveri any day.

Nuveri himself would have been the first to admit this.

Contrary to popular belief, the international fraternity of Oriental-rug dealers does not consist exclusively of wily Levantines. Admiral Christiansen, born in Red Wing, Minnesota, had a worldwide reputation. His Viking blue eyes were fading as he neared ninety, but he still regarded Paul Parajian as a rank amateur.

Lieutenant Christiansen had discovered rugs in the dim, far-off interwar Navy when a shore leave in Turkey, which should have been devoted to raki and belly dancers, went awry. Twenty lackluster years later, Commander Christiansen left the service of his country with a pension, a promotion and a passion.

He had married a Lansing girl whose father was in real estate. So, being an essentially uncomplicated man, he rented modest quarters in downtown Lansing. From there, the ripples soon reached Damascus and Istanbul.

Over the years, Parajians had grown fat and glossy from privileged Westchester matrons and *nouveau riche* corporations. But Parajians never monopolized the connoisseur market. Whenever a museum or a Rockefeller wanted a priceless Hereke, the name Christiansen was mooted. As consultant or appraiser, he was hell on wheels. In one landmark year, Christiansen locked horns with Paul Parajian over a Hamadan sold as a Herat – and won.

Admiral Christiansen knew more about aniline, chrome and vegetable dyes than anybody else west of Ankara; he knew more about the Persian wash, the London wash and the New York wash than anybody else in the world.

For decades, Paul Parajian and Homer Christiansen had co-existed in respectful hostility. Parajians avoided the deplorable practices that drew thunder from Lansing; conversely, Christiansen did not carpet a fraction of the upper-bracket Long Island estates that Parajians did.

But times change, and with them circumstances. Little by little, Parajians' wholesaling of rugs grew – first as a by-product of size, then on its own merits. Parajians' Fifth Avenue store and Fifth Avenue reputation still counted for much, but fully half the firm's revenue came from importing rugs, then distributing them to other retailers.

And, little by little, Admiral Christiansen grew old.

He himself neither recognized nor accepted this. It was Mrs Christiansen who put her foot down. She was a sunny, equable pouter pigeon of a woman who found Oriental rugs about as interesting as the peacetime Navy.

'No,' she had said one morning when Homer outlined a projected foray to Iran.

'... then on mule to Pirjond ...'

'No!' Mrs Christiansen repeated firmly.

The Admiral, accustomed to domestic acquiescence, goggled.

'You're too old to keep chasing around the way you do,' she said. 'From now on, no more of these trips ...'

It was from this clipping of the eagle's wings that détente between Christiansen and Parajian dated. Precluded from buying trips to the haunts he had made his own, Christiansen had been forced back on importers. It galled him, but did not cause him to relax his high standards. He dealt almost exclusively with Parajians.

Not that he deigned to come to New York, like lesser merchants. Imperiously, he assumed that Parajians would submit to him only choice specimens. Paul Parajian acceded to this highly unusual arrangement and routinely sent Gregory to Michigan for a variety of reasons. Matching wits with Christiansen amused him. Although he denied it, Paul had the sentimentality of his forebears for great age and great authority. And, in addition, Gregory often bought as much as he sold. Mrs Christiansen's embargo stopped at the water's edge. The Admiral still roamed widely, if by station wagon and United Airlines instead of mule. With his stupefying expertise and encyclopedic memory, he often ferreted out rugs from private hands and snapped up classics when their owners retired to Florida. Parajians always displayed a gem in its Fifth Avenue window; more than once it had passed through Homer Christiansen's hands.

'How's your father?' To all appearances, Christiansen was intent on a small Meshed as he fired off this innocuous question.

Gregory always made the Admiral dig. 'Oh, fine, fine.'

Guileless blue eyes slid rapidly over him, then back to the prayer rug.

'He's been stirring up a lot of talk. But then, he always did, even when he was just starting out. One thing I'll say for Paul. He had big ideas from the very beginning.'

Straightening arthritically, Christiansen waved aside the helping hands of several aides and continued: 'That's not a bad Meshed. Make a note of it, Susan. Number twenty-five. We'll talk about it later – if it's not overpriced, as I expect it is.'

Still talking, he led the way out of the delivery dock behind his store. What the Admiral did not accept not only went back to Parajians; it never got upstairs.

Going upstairs with the Admiral was always like walking into a meat chopper. Today, Gregory sensed, was going to be worse than usual.

'Now, what's this I hear about Parajians?' Christiansen demanded once they were in the small, shipshape office. The assistants with their note pads had all been dismissed. Christiansen did not really need reminders about any rug he had inspected in the last decade, let alone the last few hours. 'Everybody's buzzing about Paul.'

Gregory showed to best advantage when there was some distance between him and his family. Easily he said, 'What do you mean by that, Admiral?'

'You know as well as I do what I mean,' the Admiral snorted irascibly.

Gregory remained pleasantly deferential. 'Maybe you'd better tell me anyway,' he suggested.

'Mark's overseas – buying up everything that isn't nailed down,' Christiansen retorted. 'Paul sends you up here – pretending to sell me some rugs in order to take a good look around at what I might have. How much clearer could it be? You've got a big sale in mind. When's it going to be?'

Gregory was cautious. 'It's true that if we find enough first-class rugs – '

'Probably as soon as possible,' said Christiansen, ignoring him. 'Since you aren't making any secret about what Mark is doing, that means that Paul isn't letting the grass grow under his feet. Well, I don't have to tell you that I'll keep that in mind when I show you a really exceptional Herez that I've just picked up. You don't often see a deep brown like this.'

Gregory's silence did not worry Christiansen, who always conducted his most satisfactory conversations with himself.

'Of course, running around driving prices up never makes any sense. Never. And especially now – when prices are skyrocketing anyway. Still, you never know. This might be the time for a real blockbuster of a sale. Hard to tell. One thing's certain. Paul will either make a mint – or lose his shirt. There's no middle way. Don't know that I'd care to take the risk myself . . .'

He was not conscious of speaking aloud – which was why he raised his voice to a bellow when he added: 'Now, I want to be told when this sale is, young man. Not that I get around much anymore. But it might be worth my while to get to the city if I can.'

'Certainly, as soon as we know,' said Gregory, more interested in the Meshed he wanted to sell and the Herez he might want to buy.

But Christiansen was not letting him off so lightly. 'What do *you* think about it?'

'Well,' Gregory temporized, 'it's really Paul's decision.'

Christiansen examined him shrewdly. 'You don't give much away, do you?'

'Now, about that Meshed – '

'Of course, you and Mark have been putting pressure on Paul to step down, haven't you?'

Gregory stiffened. 'We'll let you know if there are any changes in the firm,' he said formally.

'You're both making a mistake – unless this sale goes wrong. Paul's got his faults, but you squeeze him out and I'll bet Parajians will go straight to hell.'

'Don't be so sure of that,' Gregory told him. 'Mark is one of the best buyers in the business! Everybody knows – '

'Oh, I don't deny that,' said the Admiral. 'Why, I remember way back when the two of them, Paul and whatsisname . . .'

'Haig,' said Gregory, gritting his teeth.

'That's right, Haig. Between the two of them, they didn't know a hill of beans about rugs – and Paul hasn't learned much since. Did I ever tell you about the time I testified in court against him? Like taking candy away from a baby.'

Fortunately, at this juncture an interruption rescued Gregory. A salesman stuck his head in the door to tell Christiansen that an old and valued customer was on the point of closing a deal for an old and valued Saraband. A few words from the great man himself would be welcomed, at least by the salesman.

Christiansen excused himself to bustle away, leaving Gregory grateful for the breather. It was a jolt to discover how much Admiral Christiansen knew – or guessed – about Parajians. Paul's sale plans were fast becoming an open secret in the trade, thanks to Mark's buying binge in the Middle East. And Christiansen's knowledge of the internal dissensions at Parajians troubled Gregory more than he cared to admit. Discovering that an outsider knew how the sides lined up at Parajians unnerved him. How much more did Christiansen know – and who had told him?

Gregory was trying to factor this new variable into an already complex situation when Christiansen returned, satisfaction leaking from every pore.

'I knew I'd get over twenty thousand for that rug, sooner or later. It was just a question of not panicking – and waiting for the right customer. Now, what were we talking about?'

Hopefully, Gregory said: 'We haven't begun to go over our consignment, Admiral. Then you said you had some rugs to show me. Paul is interested – '

Exploiting the license of extreme age, Christiansen rejected Gregory's evasion and resumed his reminiscences. 'That's right,' he told himself. 'Paul and that brother of his. What I was saying was – you and Mark don't have the flair. You make your father step down and you'll regret it.'

'I can't imagine where you picked up this information, but – '

'No, Paul is going to stay at Parajians until they carry him out,' said the Admiral with disinterested objectivity. 'And that shouldn't be for a while, should it?'

Gregory looked sharply at him, then decided that his ears had deceived him. This was nothing more than senile humor.

The next two hours should have taught him better. By the time they had plowed through the consignment from Parajians and the two magnificent silk Tabrizes that Christiansen was offering, Gregory was sweating. The Admiral, if anything, was more beatific than usual.

'Not a bad day's work,' he commented while secretaries typed bills of sale.

'For you, anyway,' said Gregory aridly.

The Admiral treated this as a pleasantry. 'For both of us, I hope. Of course, you'll have to wait and see, won't you? It'll all depend on how Paul's sale goes. And a lot of people find waiting the hardest part. Well, give my best to your father. Tell him I wish him all the luck in the world.'

But even before Gregory could reply with conventional cordiality, Christiansen added a stinger: 'From what I hear, he'll need it!'

'My luck is changing, Harriet,' Paul Parajian said expansively. 'I tell you, I can feel it in my bones.'

She put the tray down and topped up his ritual predinner Scotch. Only then did she reply: 'Oh, you do, do you?'

The glint of mockery roused him. 'I know you think I get carried away. But things are changing. We're already getting calls about the auction – and that's got to be a good sign. And Mark has been picking up some real beauties. Gregory hasn't done badly with Christiansen, either.' He paused, swirled his glass, then confided: 'You know, both the boys are really co-operating. It's been a big load off my mind. If they were digging in their heels right now ...'

Reminding herself to send Sara something nice, Harriet held her peace.

'So I'm feeling pretty optimistic, all things considered.'

This was nothing new. Long ago, Harriet had realized that Paul was so buoyant he needed a guy line tethering him to solid ground.

'That's fine as far as it goes,' she said affectionately. 'Just don't forget Veron's murder. Or this wrangle about control. Or – '

'I know, I know,' he interrupted, his spirits unquenched. 'But time will take care of all that.'

'I suppose it will,' she agreed readily. 'But still, the best decision I ever made was to send Steve to camp in Colorado this summer.'

'I miss him,' said Paul simply.

Harriet frequently accused her husband of doting on the child of his old age, so she spoke bracingly: 'It's worked out better than we expected.'

Last June, with a major family fight brewing, fourteen-year-old Stephen Parajian had been dispatched to a summer of horses and canoes. Not a day went by without Harriet's giving thanks that he was so far away from murder and police investigations.

'And he's learning all the techniques for survival in the wilderness,' she quoted dutifully.

Paul was a fond, but not a foolish parent. 'Bah!' he snorted. 'Wait until he starts buying rugs. He'll learn some survival techniques those cowboys have never heard of.'

9. Youth's Sweet-Scented Manuscript

Haggling is not synonymous with *suqs*, Muslims and endless cups of Turkish coffee. It is not only hammered copper trays and Kurdish saddlebags that necessitate hard bargaining.

John Thatcher was dealing with Godleigh Flatware, Inc., that fine old New England firm, when Miss Corsa entered the office and hovered meaningfully.

'Yes, Butterworth,' Thatcher told the phone for the fourth time. 'We do approve of conservative accounting. But you seem to be denying the existence of your silver inventory – '

Butterworth's indignation was audible even to Miss Corsa, but Thatcher persisted: ' – and while the Sloan is always available for legitimate business financing, we do not intend to bankroll a series of proxy fights against all comers.'

Butterworth exuded puritan virtue, then promised to check with the board and get back to Thatcher.

'I'll be happy to talk to you,' said Thatcher, redeeming this untruth by adding: 'if you feel able to rethink your position. Yes, Miss Corsa?'

'Mr Gabler would like to see you for a few moments, if it is convenient,' she announced.

Thatcher had no personal inclination for the shirt-sleeve style of office management; more to the point, neither did Miss Corsa. Still, the comings and goings of such senior staff as Everett Gabler and Charlie Trinkam were not usually accorded full honors. So, putting Godleigh Flatware from his mind, he looked up inquiringly.

Miss Corsa obliged. 'A Mrs Daniels is with him.'

'Mrs Daniels? Good God, the Parajians again! Well, I suppose you'd better tell him to bring her along.'

Thatcher, who sidestepped energy czars and Swedish economists with ease, was accommodating not a Parajian, but Gabler. Requests for a formal audience, especially when blessed by Miss Corsa, were not to be lightly dismissed.

But was there any need for Everett to behave as if this were a levee of the Sun King?

'Ah, John. I'm happy that you were able to give us a few moments. As I've already explained, you will certainly have to participate in our decision. You do remember Mrs Daniels, don't you?'

Thatcher was pleased to see Sara Daniels unawed by this show of force.

Repudiating the role of petitioner, she broke into Everett's speech: 'But all I'm asking for is an advance, Mr Gabler. People must do it all the time!'

People did, and Everett was condemning the practice when Sara turned the tables on him by addressing herself directly to Thatcher: 'You explained why you have to hold up distributing Aunt Veron's stock in Parajians,' she said earnestly. 'And I haven't come to argue about that. But she left a lot of money, too. Sooner or later, Mark and Gregory and I are going to get it. And it isn't as if I were asking for all of our share. Just, say, twenty-five thousand dollars.'

Did that slight falter indicate ebbing confidence, or anxiety? Thatcher could not tell. Many Parajians, he suddenly realized, had talked about Veron Aratounian's company stock. Sara was the first to evince interest in all those dividends that had been piling up.

'As Mr Gabler has no doubt already explained – '

'Mr Gabler said that the Sloan would have to think about it,' said Sara with a grimace. 'That won't do me much good. The reason that I'm asking for an advance is because I need the money now, Mr Thatcher.'

There was an echo of Paul Parajian in this forthright statement, and Thatcher replied in kind.

'Then I'm afraid it has to be *no*,' he said. 'So long as any doubt about Mrs Aratounian's identity exists – '

'Damn Lois!' Mrs Daniels said bitterly.

' – any distribution is impossible. We have to be satisfied that the owner of this estate is not still alive.'

Looking disappointed, Sara bit her lip thoughtfully.

'I was afraid you'd say that,' she said almost to herself. 'But it was worth a try.'

Thatcher, if not Everett, was amused by this confession.

'Do you have any idea how long it will take – before you find out about Veron?' she asked matter-of-factly.

There was nothing Everett liked better than describing the scope and intensity of the Sloan's actions in this area. Since Thatcher had already heard it several times, he was free to contemplate the young woman before him.

Mrs Daniels was candid about her need for money, which Thatcher marked a point in her favor. For every lie told about sex, there are a thousand told about dollars. But frankness is a technique that can conceal as much as it reveals.

'... records from the immigration authorities in Greece in the twenties, before the Aratounians returned to Soviet Armenia,' Everett was saying. 'I regret to say that those records leave much to be desired – '

'They've had other things to do in the Balkans besides perfect their files,' Thatcher commented.

Sara was appalled. 'But that will take years!'

'Not at all,' said Everett. 'We do recognize the need for reasonable dispatch. In a matter of weeks – '

Sara was not wasting time on lost causes. 'That's terribly disappointing,' she said, without heat. 'But anyway, I do appreciate your taking time to see me.'

Or, as Everett put it upon returning from the elevator: 'A very pleasant contrast to Mrs Gregory Parajian.'

'And a very easy young woman to underestimate,' said Thatcher. 'I wonder if her father or her brothers – or her husband, for that matter – knew she was coming to see us.'

'I will try to find out,' said Everett unexpectedly. 'The reason I came back, John, is to explain why I brought Mrs Daniels along. I know you want to keep abreast of developments in the whole Parajian situation – '

'I know why you brought her in here,' said Thatcher dryly.

Everett would not be drawn.

' – so you ought to know Commercial Credit has extended Paul Parajian's loan by three hundred fifty thousand dollars –'

'Good Lord! I hope they know what they're doing.'

' – so, representing Veron Aratounian or her heirs, I propose talking to Paul Parajian in greater detail about his immediate plans. I had not fully grasped how ambitious they are. At any rate, I wondered if you would be interested in accompanying me.'

Thatcher's courteous but unambiguous refusal was stillborn when Miss Corsa entered with an unwelcome reminder from the president of the Sloan Guaranty Trust:

'You won't forget that Mr Withers wants you to join him at Lincoln Center for the conference on business support for cultural activities in New York?'

When it came to a choice between rug merchants and the performing arts, Thatcher was no better than the next man.

'Yes,' he said with alacrity that deceived no one. 'Yes, it might be interesting to go over and chat with Paul Parajian.'

At Parajians, the salesman was surprised they even had to ask.

'He's down at the docks,' he explained, nipping off the *of course* just in time. When he grasped how woefully ignorant they were, he made things even simpler. 'Mr Mark Parajian has been on a buying trip in the Middle East. The first of his shipments arrived this morning, so Mr Paul Parajian – '

Testily, Everett extracted precise directions.

Thatcher did not protest. With the Metropolitan Opera and *its* eccentric approach to accounting as his alternative, even an August afternoon on the docks was acceptable. Furthermore, Everett was perfectly capable of transacting business there. He had, Thatcher knew to his cost, the unforgiving tenacity of the beaver.

But you can't build dams without sticks. Paul Parajian was not at the Lower West Side pier either.

'No, you just missed him,' said Barney Olender when they

finally ran him to ground in Warehouse C. 'Of course, he'll be back in an hour or two, if you want to wait. We've got a lot to do here. The *Mustafa Bey* just put in this morning.'

'A lot to do' sounded like an understatement to Thatcher. They were standing in a cement-floored shed that absorbed heat like a sponge. Around them were thick, baled rolls containing ten to twelve rugs each, with hefty longshoremen dumping others in an unending stream. Near the door, a small table, covered with documents, served as a makeshift desk.

Everett, always single-minded when he got on the trail, was ready to leave, but Thatcher felt inclined to linger.

Nor was it the treasures of the fabled East that detained him.

Years ago, when the upper echelons of the U.S. Government had lapsed into permanent insanity, Thatcher had consoled himself by recalling that the same bureaucracy harbors thousands of capable employees, getting on with the job while all around them lose their heads. There are also hundreds of true experts whose mere existence is a bulwark against national disaster. Unfortunately, civil servants are the shyest of creatures, lurking deep within the Bureau of Weights and Measures, the Park Service or the Treasury, and rarely sighted far afield. But here, right on the New York Port Authority's docks, were two customs men who knew more about Oriental rugs than anybody at the Metropolitan Museum. They joined Barney in genial contempt for a job lot of Hamadans, outdid him in admiring two spectacular Qums, then got down to brass tacks. The object of their immediate attention was a prayer rug. It was old; it was valuable; and it was possible, barely possible, that it might qualify for the antique exemption.

'I would have put it in the eighteen eighties, myself,' Barney said righteously.

No, no, they told him politely. A snap decision might put it in the eighties, but a good case could be made for the sixties. With this, the conversation became heavily technical. Since it centered largely on warps and woofs, the outsider felt he was listening to furry animals barking at each other. But Thatcher was left with the comfortable assurance that the nation's customs revenues were in good hands, which was more than he could say for its oil-depletion allowances.

Once the prayer rug was sped on its way, a natural break occurred. The U.S. Customs produced thermos bottles of strong coffee, and Olender returned to his visitors. His apologetic attitude was not, it developed, a result of Paul Parajian's absence.

'I wouldn't want you to think that most of these are for *us*,' he said, conjuring up a Cartier salesman confronted with a Mickey Mouse watch. 'They'll be going wholesale.'

Everett had his standards too. 'Parajians' wholesaling is highly successful – or so I understand. But you're surely not planning to wholesale that prayer rug, are you?'

Although Olender's look of alarm was almost ludicrous, it roused Everett's darkest suspicions. Thatcher felt required to intervene.

'We have heard about Parajians' plans for a major sale, you know,' he pointed out. 'As you may know, quite apart from the information we have ... er, amassed in connection with Mrs Aratounian's estate, the Sloan has been involved in financing Mark Parajian's trip.'

'Oh, sure, sure,' said Olender quickly. 'It's just that – well, I'm getting pretty tired of everybody second-guessing Paul! Hell, he built this business from nothing. Now everybody knows better than he does.'

Thatcher tried to smooth the hackles they had inadvertently raised. 'Sons don't always appreciate their fathers' achievements,' he said. 'They only see the end result.'

Barney might have been hearing this platitude for the first time.

'You're right,' he said eagerly. 'Do you know how Paul started? His first address was a garage, where he was hacking a cab. People left a message and he called back when he got in from his run. He operated that way for a couple of years. For Christ's sake, his first regular phone was in the hall of some boardinghouse in Brooklyn. That was after Haig came over. Paul went on hacking, his brother pushed a cart on the Lower East Side and between them they covered the phone. They were saving every cent – and why? Because war was in the air. They figured if they could get just one shipment of good rugs over, they'd have it made. And they were right. After Paul sold that first lot, he never looked back.'

'I gather you've been with Parajians for a long time,' said Thatcher, incurring a glance from Everett Gabler that was worthy of Miss Corsa.

'Since 1939,' Olender said proudly. 'Paul moved into my rooming house after his brother got killed in that accident. At the beginning, I just helped. He took one of those defense jobs, and I happened to have some spare time. So, little by little, I did more of the dog work. Hell, that was the first shipment I cleared through customs for him.' He broke off to look around the cavernous shed. 'I never thought I'd go on doing it so long. Anyway, after Pearl Harbor, Paul went into the army. You know he ended up as one of their consultants on looted rugs in Germany, don't you? With my bum ticker, they wouldn't have me. So I kept things going. We've been together ever since.'

'Then, in a real sense,' Thatcher remarked, 'Parajians is your accomplishment too.'

Olender stepped aside to let three men lug a long cylinder past. 'Oh, I wouldn't say that,' he said, blinking slightly. 'Sure, I'm proud of the way things have gone. But not the way Paul is. You see, I sort of fell into this. Paul starved and scraped for it. Why, when I first met him ...'

He paused over some internal system of timekeeping. Then, with his right hand marking the beat, he whistled a few bars of 'My Heart Belongs to Daddy.' 'Yup, that's when it was. I'd never seen an Oriental rug then, and I didn't understand what he was talking about.'

Still beating time, he fell into silent contemplation of the past.

Everett did not like loose ends. 'Subsequently, however –'

'No!' said Olender with unexpected firmness, struggling for the right words. 'People don't split a gut unless they have a dream. And it has to be your own dream, not somebody else's. That's the only thing that keeps you going through one-night stands and cheap hotels and sitting up on the train.'

'When did Paul Parajian do all this?' asked Everett baffled.

'Paul? Who's talking about Paul? I'm talking about *me*. That was back in the thirties when I had my own combo.' Reflexively, he began keying an invisible clarinet. 'Those were the days. Every one of us was going to have the biggest band the country had ever seen, with full houses, and people coming for miles. That's the way it was, you know. And when the music was coming right, you could make yourself believe it was going to happen – hell, that it was happening.'

As he spoke, they were all transported backward through time. Then Olender shook himself. 'But the war came and closed the roadhouses. That's why I was out of work when Paul needed someone. So I went into Oriental rugs, and I made a bundle. But you can't ever say that it's been the same for me as it was for Paul.'

'No,' said Thatcher. 'I see what you mean.'

Everett Gabler was made of sterner stuff. 'Then you and Mr Khassim are the only outsiders who have been involved in Parajians.'

'Oh, Khassim,' said Barney, in a voice that spoke volumes. Almost immediately, he looked regretful. 'Well, I'm afraid I've got to get back to work. I'll tell Paul you want to see him.'

But before returning to the customs men, he had to deliver himself: 'If you're paying attention to Khassim or any of the rest of them, you're barking up the wrong tree. Paul says that old lady was Veron – and he doesn't have any reason to lie. You just think about it!'

With that, he dived back into a pile of disputed Bakhtiaris as if hotly pursued.

'Interesting,' commented Thatcher when he had dislodged Gabler. 'I wonder what the rub with Khassim is.'

'Jealousy, no doubt,' said Gabler, who was always ready with a discreditable motive.

'That's possible, of course,' said Thatcher. 'But it might be more. Khassim, after all, is identified with an area of Parajian's life that has been mysterious from the start – the discovery of the children and the introduction of Mrs Aratounian. And there is no doubt where Olender's loyalty lies.'

'Which simply means,' said Gabler, 'that all his observations are tainted with bias.'

'I wasn't thinking about observations,' said Thatcher. 'I was thinking about actions.'

When Gabler projected disapproval, he defended himself. 'No, Everett, this is not a flight of fancy. After all, Olender and Khassim were the only outsiders present at the lunch with Mrs Aratounian – as I expect the police have already noted.'

Everett mulled this over and came up with a dispiriting conclusion. 'Everybody is suspect. I have been working on that assumption throughout, John. The Sloan is going to spare no efforts – '

'In any event,' Thatcher said hastily, 'there really isn't any doubt about Olender's truthfulness when he explains his own relationship to the firm. Perhaps that lets him out, Everett. To hear him talk, rugs still take second place to bands.'

For once Everett did not cavil. 'Quite extraordinary how he brought back that period for me. I had quite forgotten.'

Thatcher nodded.

Barney Olender's mastery of language was imperfect, but he had performed the Proustian miracle anyway. Thatcher was no romantic about the thirties; nobody on Wall Street is. If you had asked him what that era meant, he would have cited bread lines, foreclosures and bankruptcies. And Everett was not romantic about anything. But as they stood outside the customs shed looking vainly for a cab, both men fell silent, recalling something lost in the mists of youth – a clear, haunting sliver of sound piercing the night.

Briefly Everett forgot he was a banker.

'You know,' he said, 'they don't make music the way they used to.'

10. The Moving Finger

John Thatcher and Everett Gabler could follow their fancy – even to the West Side docks. More junior members of the Sloan were well advised to stick closer to home. As too many people forget, the most critical ingredient of success is being there when they want you.

So Ken Nicolls was there on a muggy Saturday morning, doggedly reading the last draft of a report before signing it. But it was midsummer. Vacation was not only in the Sloan air, it had already started for everybody in the Nicolls family except the breadwinner. And last-minute chores were making it impossible for him to spend the weekend on Cape Cod.

When Ken finally grounded his pen, he found himself facing empty hours in a stifling city. The life of a temporary bachelor is not all that it is cracked up to be. He could go home and clean the basement of his brownstone in Brooklyn Heights. He could continue the unending search for those small screws to hold the doorknob plate on the closet door. He could ... Suddenly a long-dormant ambition burst into life.

'That's what I'll do,' he said aloud, his voice a hollow echo on the empty sixth floor of the Sloan.

The firm of Parajians had more than one link with the Trust Department. Last year, for instance, the executor's final accounting in the estate of Mrs James Longwood had declared that the Sloan Guaranty Trust had employed Paul Parajian to appraise several Oriental rugs. Naturally, no mention was made of the humble details surrounding this transaction. Ken Nicolls had been sent out with the key to the Longwood house in Manhasset. There he had met Arthur Sourian, who took the rugs back to Parajians for appraisal and shipment to Mrs Longwood's daughter in Seattle. But that meeting had left its mark.

'They're beauties, aren't they?' Ken had said as he watched the rugs being rolled up.

Sourian was more technical. 'Mrs Longwood should have had us clean them a long time ago,' he said severely, stooping to pick up a tangle of gray matter. 'Dog hair!'

'Oh!' Ken was struck by a new thought. 'I suppose dogs are a problem with Orientals.'

'No, no!' The answer burst forth like a reflex. Everybody in the rug business has learned a hard lesson. If any dealer is silly enough to suggest that either the Bokhara goes or little Schnappsie goes, he will have a fine Bokhara back on his hands – pronto! 'Most people who have Orientals also have dogs.'

In fact, Sourian explained, the two seemed to go together. The same Longwood daughter who was taking the rugs as part of her inheritance had also chosen to house her mother's two Old English sheep dogs.

'Someday,' Ken had confided, reassured about his beagle, 'I'd like to have a rug like that.'

Not surprisingly, Ken had left Manhasset with Arthur Sourian's card. He had not forgotten that conversation.

Neither, it developed an hour later, had Sourian.

'Why, Mr Nicolls!' he said, before Ken had advanced ten paces into the Parajian showroom. 'Are you interested in anything in particular?'

Despite his resolve to buy Jane the rug of his dreams, Ken was overcome by a wave of self-consciousness. 'Well . . . that is . . . I thought I'd look around.'

At Parajians, salesmanship was a fine art.

'Of course!' With a wave Sourian placed two thousand rugs at Ken's feet. 'Why don't you get an idea first of what we have?'

The next half hour was an education for Ken. On the minus side was the growing conviction that he knew less about rugs than anyone else in the room – salesmen, customers, bystanders. On the plus side was the reassurance that he had not strayed into a feminine domain. The few women dotted about the place were patiently waiting for their husbands. But it was the men who were the enthusiasts. They were the ones discoursing knowledgeably; they were the ones flipping to the back of a rug to examine its underside and, in the penultimate moments of a sale, they were the ones who got down on their hands and knees to crawl lovingly over every square inch. One of them was just getting up now.

'A real honey!' he announced, dusting his trousers.

'Yes, indeed, Dr Allen,' beamed the salesman. 'And not a bad price.'

For the first time, the doctor's wife spoke from the sidelines. 'Seventeen thousand dollars?' she inquired dispassionately.

Her husband misinterpreted the interjection. 'Pretty good, isn't it? I wouldn't have expected to get it for a penny less than twenty thousand. When can you deliver?'

'We could lay it for you on Wednesday. And while I'm having the bill of sale drawn up, I know Mr Parajian would like to speak with you himself about that fringe.'

Ken was never able to figure out what mysterious system of communication produced Paul Parajian and Barney Olender before Mrs Allen was well into her second embittered sentence. But he was glad to see two men about whom he was curious, as well as the Parajian system at work.

Here it was the buyer who gushed over the quality of the wares and the seller who gravely listed defects.

'It's a pity that the original fringe was removed at some time,' Paul Parajian lamented, 'but they haven't done a bad job matching the new one.'

'Even when you've been told, you can't see the difference,' agreed his customer.

Dr Allen had certainly been told. Not only had his salesman labored the point, but a large tag with heavy block printing underlined the warning. Parajians was proud of its reputation for candor, and rightly so. That reputation was worth a mint.

Paul Parajian proceeded from esthetics to history. 'We regard ourselves as lucky to have acquired that rug. My son tells me that when he saw it in the bazaar in Tabriz . . .'

But his finest moment came with the pacification of Mrs Allen. Almost casually Paul elicited her present décor, then became one connoisseur talking to another. 'Ah, that explains it.

Ordinarily, you see, we sell this rug in stronger tones. The subtler coloring is lost on the great majority of buyers, just as the lines of your French furniture would be. They prefer the starkness, almost the primitiveness, of contemporary Danish. It requires a more sophisticated discrimination to appreciate ...'

At this juncture Ken, lurking in the background, was startled to see Dr Allen solemnly wink at him. Clearly, in certain circles it was well known that Paul gave value for the money.

What was more, he enjoyed doing it. House policy probably demanded the luster of Paul Parajian's presence for sales over a certain figure. That made plenty of commercial sense. But it was not an onerous duty. Ken could see that Parajian was relishing every moment with the Allens. Surely this must be what he had been dreaming about when he stepped off Ellis Island or even when he opened his first small store. Not that there was any hint of this background now. As he made courtly farewells to Mrs Allen, he looked like a man who had been born a success.

'Mr Olender will arrange the delivery for you,' he was saying as he shook hands. 'Barney, I have to take Harriet to lunch. You'll be sure that the men have instructions about the underlayment.'

'Leave it to me, Paul,' Barney chirped cheerfully. 'Now, Mrs Allen, you say there's a concert grand piano and a Directoire breakfront to be moved?'

Ken would have welcomed further information about the Allen investment in nest-building, but Arthur Sourian felt that he had let the hook dangle long enough. 'Well, Mr Nicolls,' he said, materializing from nowhere. 'Have you seen anything you liked?'

There was nothing to lose. 'I sure have,' he admitted. 'That!'

That was a Sarouk, gleaming on the wall like a Rembrandt. It cost fifty-seven thousand dollars.

'And,' Ken went on doggedly, 'I was thinking of spending about eight or nine hundred dollars.'

Sourian had met this challenge many times before. 'Let's forget about price for the moment,' he suggested. 'I want to find out the kind of pattern that interests you. That Sarouk is a medallion design, not an allover. If you would come this way, I'd like to show you something.'

When their goal turned out to be seven thousand dollars' worth of Kerman, Ken asked himself if Arthur Sourian could be under any illusion about the Nicolls role at the Sloan. It was key-carrier and house-opener, not chairman of the board.

'I know it's too expensive for you, but tell me frankly what you think of it.'

'I don't like it as well as the Sarouk.'

'Ah!' Sourian acted as if they were now hot on the trail of victory. 'That's all I wanted to know. We can forget the Kermans. Now, over here I have something that may surprise you.'

But Ken was not the only one destined for surprises that day. Blocking their path and apparently deaf to Sourian's gentle 'Excuse me' was Barney Olender. He was staring at a figure coming through the front door as if he were seeing a ghost.

'Hector!' he said to himself in a doubting whisper before raising his voice to tones rarely heard on that showroom floor. 'Hector! I thought you were in Teheran!'

'Ah, Barney!' The portly figure swerved from its course toward the elevator. 'I was, I was. But quite unexpectedly, I found I have unfinished business here at Parajians.'

Barney gulped, looked wildly around for assistance, then fell back on the conventions. 'I sure didn't expect to see you, but it's great to have you back. We don't see enough of you, Hector.'

'I was hoping to catch Paul before he went out to lunch,' Khassim said meaningfully.

'Then we'd better step on it. I think Harriet's picking him up.' Barney had fallen into step beside the unexpected visitor.

'You must not let me take you from your work.'

'I was just going upstairs myself. And I wouldn't miss this for the world.'

Unknown to Barney, Harriet had already arrived and was shepherding her husband through the last-minute details that routinely delayed their lunches.

'I just have one call to make, then we can leave right away,'

Paul was saying as he threw open a door. 'It will only take a min . . . What the hell!'

If he was taken aback, so were the occupants of the office. Mark and Gregory had been reinforced by Lois and Sara and Alex. For all practical purposes, Paul had just strayed into a smoke-filled room.

It was unfortunate that Lois, her back to the door, serenely insisted on finishing her sentence before turning to see what had startled the others.

'. . . and you have to admit that it's unfair that he takes a bigger salary out of the company, when Gregory works so much harder.'

Grimly Paul halted at the threshold and examined his children. But Harriet, drifting to a seat and settling herself, merely remarked, 'How nice to find you all here.'

Untouched by embarrassment, Lois seized on the inaccuracy. 'We're not all here. Helen couldn't be bothered to come in from Amagansett.'

Mark defended his wife. 'She has enough sense to realize she doesn't know a damned thing about business!'

With the ease born of practice, Harriet ignored this unpleasantness. 'And Helen must be terribly busy anyway, with Corinne's wedding around the corner. You'll see how hectic that can be, Lois, when it's time to marry off your own daughter.'

Paul Parajian knew that Harriet was trying to remind everybody of family ties, future as well as present. But he had his own way of doing things.

'Still trying to figure out how to pressure me?' he demanded baldly. 'I advise you to forget it. This delay at the Sloan is your fault – not mine. Now, if you want to do something useful, let's talk about the sale. The Parke-Bernet people have set the date . . .'

Irritably he broke off as brisk footsteps neared the door he had neglected to close behind him.

'Say, folks, you'll never guess who's back,' yodeled Barney Olender. 'It's Hector. Just like the bad penny that keeps turning up!'

Like the old trouper that he was, Barney did not let his own emotions color his performance, but in seconds audience feed-back had its effect. As a result, his introduction weakened steadily. 'Well, the more the merrier, I always say!'

Merriment was conspicuously absent. Only Harriet could manage a normal greeting.

Khassim retained his aplomb. 'But I see that I am interrupting a conference. I can always – '

'Hector!' Mark Parajian was openly accusing. 'I left you three days ago – and you didn't say anything about coming to New York.'

'It was a last-minute decision. Something unexpected came up, something that I must take care of. But, of course, it can wait. At the moment, I am intruding.'

Barney always liked to smooth over the rough spots. 'Oh, no, we're all old friends here.'

No one seconded him.

'Sometimes,' said Khassim blandly, 'you discover you are not such old friends as you mistakenly thought.'

Nuances were lost on Lois. 'Well, we are having a conference,' she said flat-footedly. 'And after all, you aren't one of the family.'

Somebody sucked in his breath, but Khassim simply smiled. 'My dear Lois,' he said, ignoring her expression. 'You become more of a Parajian every day. So concerned about family. It is a wonderful thing in women. Look at Veron. Such a devoted sister, so close to her oldest brother – yet willing to be a devoted aunt as well.'

'What do you mean by that?' Daniels asked truculently.

'Poor Veron! One cannot help wondering if she would not be alive today – had she been less close to her beloved family!'

Audibly, Gregory choked over a retort.

'That's enough, Hector,' said Paul, half amused as he watched the expert baiting of his children. 'Perhaps you wouldn't mind waiting until we finish up in here. You can take a look at the auction catalog. Barney, ask Miss Martineau to take care of Hector. Then' – he paused significantly – 'then you come back.'

'Oh, look, Paul!' Barney protested.

'You're a stockholder,' Paul said.

'A stockholder who'll do just what you tell him,' Lois cried hotly.

Harriet did some mild chiding as Hector Khassim was swept away. 'I expect that's why Paul wants him here, Lois.'

'Good God, nobody cares if Barney sits in!' Mark was still scowling at the door. 'But Hector's the one I'm glad to see out of the way. There's something fishy about this sudden trip of his.'

'Of course there is,' said Paul Parajian, impatiently. 'You know what Hector's like! He knows about the trouble here, and he wants to take advantage of it. Don't worry, we'll find out what he's up to soon enough. But you wanted to get rid of him so you could talk sense to me. Well, go ahead!'

Downstairs, Arthur Sourian did not need any such invitation.

'... a floral spray that shows to good effect against ivory. The design is similar to that Joshigan we looked at.'

'Yes,' said Ken fatalistically.

Unlike Paul Parajian's family, Sourian valued the use of silence. He let the floral spray speak for itself, then uncovered a Karaja.

'Now, if you prefer a red field, we have this lovely pattern of geometric medallions.'

Ken's eyes were slightly glazed. Protracted nonstop rug viewing is guaranteed to reduce the neophyte to total confusion about color, size and design – if not price. At Parajians, they knew all about the financial equivalent of the bends, as well as the rapture of the deep. Ken had already been decompressed from fifty-seven thousand dollars to seven thousand dollars. Now Sourian was using floral sprays and geometric medallions as a thirty-five-hundred-dollar resting stage.

'Now, this Kasvin may interest you. It has a nice, simple border ...'

Ken was inspecting the nice, simple border when a shrill dehumanized shriek cut through the air like a knife.

'My God!' he gasped. 'What's that?'

Sourian could only stutter.

But it was a woman somewhere, screaming.

Briefly, this nightmare sound congealed the whole showroom – freezing salesmen midway through graceful gestures; turning shoppers into figures out of Madame Tussaud's. Then movement resumed. There was a rush to the stairway that led to the balcony.

Ken found himself neck and neck with another salesman, taking the stairs two at a time. Breathless, they reached the balcony to find a knot of people already outside an office.

'What is it? What's happened? Who was that screaming?' Paul Parajian shoved past Ken with rough authority.

'Mr Parajian!' the man nearest the door gulped, relieved yet fearful. 'Miss Martineau found him. I mean, something seems to have happened to Mr Khassim. I've called the ambulance.'

With one stride, Parajian pushed forward to thrust the door wide. At one side of the room, with two co-workers supporting her, sagged the sobbing Miss Martineau. Opposite them, Hector Khassim lay sprawled across the desk, his arms outstretched, his head twisted sideways. He was totally still. Spittle from the corner of his mouth was already glazing.

Miss Martineau struggled upright. 'Oh, Mr Parajian,' she wailed. 'He's dead now. But before he died, he said he was poisoned ... poisoned ... poisoned ...'

11. Past Regrets and Future Fears

Like everybody else on the balcony, Ken Nicolls was overwhelmed, almost paralyzed. But memory is a capricious censor. Long after horror and shock fade, inconsequential detail will remain. What Ken would never forget was the muttered comment of someone behind him.

'One thing I'll say. If you've got to get yourself killed, Fifth Avenue's the place to do it.'

For one numbing moment, this seemed to be another ill-timed attempt at black humor. Then all heads were jerked away from the room where Hector Khassim lay dead toward the two-story plate-glass windows at the front of the building. Sirens, flashing blue lights and, as Ken stared, more squad cars.

By the time the first policemen pounded indoors, the initial shock was fading.

'Barney,' said Paul Parajian, trying to control his voice. 'I don't think we should have all these people standing around here.'

But the police were not hanging back to let order reassert itself. On the contrary, they introduced their own discipline with practiced rapidity. While two uniformed men strode wordlessly into the office, a third stationed himself outside the closed door.

'Okay,' he said tersely. 'First of all, will everybody please keep quiet while I ask some questions? What's the victim's name?'

'Khassim. Mr Hector – '

'Khassim? How do you spell it?'

Rapid-fire question, answer and note-taking continued for several minutes. At the end of that interval, Ken was standing aside with customers, salesmen and a few other strays. A smaller group was being shepherded into an office down the hallway.

'It's going to be a helluva lot more interesting in there with the big shots,' a chatty salesman remarked as they trudged downstairs. 'If anybody had a knife out for Khassim, it was the family – two to one.'

A flying wedge of technical experts separated Ken from his companion, so he did not reply. The comment did, however, trigger a pang of doubt. He might be relieved at not joining the inner circle, but what about Everett Gabler? The Sloan liked to see its men where the action was.

To hell with them, he thought in a confused spasm of self-assertion. If they want me in hot spots, they're going to have to pay me more.

Ken was not the only one to fall prey to dark musings. A lady customer was burning with resentment.

'We could have walked out,' she informed their official escort. 'Let me tell you, that's what a lot of people did. I must have seen a dozen people racing outside, as soon as the screaming started!'

'Yes, ma'am.'

'And that's what I would have done, but could I find Irving? No, I could not. And why? Because you were looking at another Gul! Because you've got to look at Guls, we sit here – like criminals.'

The unfortunate Irving was let off the hook by the arrival of a detective. Almost at once, he uncovered interesting, if small, anomalies.

'Now, I understand that none of you folks knew this Hector Khassim ...'

Ken found himself nodding agreement to this suggestion as vehemently as Irving, but another quarter demurred.

'We-ell,' said Arthur Sourian reluctantly. 'I suppose you could say that I *knew* him ...'

Flushing, he registered Detective Williams' curiosity and speeded up his defense. '... that is to say, I had met him a couple of times. That's all.'

Williams said only, 'Did you talk to him today?'

'God, no! Mr Nicolls here can tell you that Khassim and Barney were too busy. And so was I!'

Fortunately, with the ice broken, other salesmen were emboldened. They too had all met Hector Khassim at one time or another, and several of them had witnessed his encounter with Barney Olender.

'Ye-es,' said an older man with massive discretion. 'Barney did look a little surprised.'

Ken had already been exposed to the big mouth of the sales force. Now it was the police's turn.

'What do you mean, surprised?' rallied the salesman who had offered two-to-one on the family. 'Barney was ready to drop his teeth. He looked as if he had seen a ghost!'

Detective Williams pounced. 'Cox,' he told a subordinate. 'Take Mr Muir upstairs. The captain'll want to talk to him.'

Mr Muir was led away, looking as if he had bitten into a persimmon. Thereafter anticlimax prevailed until they got to names, addresses and permission to leave. Or, in some cases, orders.

'No,' said Williams, frowning at his own hieroglyphics. 'You go on home. The store's closed for the day.'

'Are those Mr Paul Parajian's instructions?' Sourian wanted to know.

Williams smiled sourly. 'Those are the Police Commissioner's instructions. Mr Paul Parajian's otherwise occupied.'

Detective Williams was putting it mildly. Even the preliminaries were worse upstairs. Downstairs the police had got to Ken Nicolls and his companions within ten minutes. In Paul Parajian's office, ten minutes stretched into twenty, twenty-five and more.

'Can't somebody keep her quiet?' Gregory asked tightly.

'She can't help it,' Harriet admonished him.

In the corner, Miss Martineau sobbed with metronomic regularity. Trying to comfort her was the office manager. A white-faced typist sat nearby staring blankly into space.

The presence of outsiders discouraged conversation. When Paul Parajian did speak, everybody jumped.

'Where's Alex?' he asked, for the sake of saying something.

Mark nodded meaningfully toward Miss Martineau, but Sara responded readily: 'He had to leave, right after our meeting.'

'Ah.' Parajian nodded, not much interested.

Just then Lois looked up. 'Right after our meeting? I thought I saw him – '

'Lois!'

Gregory's hand descended on his wife's shoulder as Mark clumsily weighed in: 'I think it would be better for all of us to save this for the police, when they come.'

Once again, Harriet exerted herself in the interest of neutrality.

'I wonder if they ever will come,' she remarked as lightly as she could. 'We seem to have been here forever.'

Her contribution nearly backfired. Miss Martineau's sobs grew louder. With an oath, Paul Parajian started for the door.

'Paul!'

'Listen, Dad ...'

But Parajian was forestalled. The door was already opening to reveal Captain Muller.

'Sorry you had to wait,' he said coolly. 'But when Headquarters got the call from Parajians, they alerted me. Then, once the boys saw what you've got for me this time' – Lois was not the only one to shudder – 'I was on my way.'

'We understand,' Paul Parajian forced himself to reply. 'After Veron – well, it's only natural. We'll do everything we can to cooperate with you, Captain Muller.'

But Muller did not show much interest in cooperation. After a quick survey, he gave instructions that sped Miss Martineau, the typist and the office manager to other hands. The Parajians and Barney Olender he was keeping for himself.

'Okay,' he said, as if Paul Parajian had never spoken. 'It looks like poison again. You haven't been careless about leaving your pills around again, have you, Mr Olender?'

Barney's response was a ghastly smile and an instinctive hand clapped against his breast pocket. 'No, they're here.'

Muller gave him an odd look. 'It's early days for that. We'll wait until the doctor's report. Right now, let's get started on what we do know. They tell me Khassim walked into the store at noon. You damn near passed out when you caught sight of him, Mr Olender.'

'No, no,' Barney croaked. 'I don't know who told you that. But I was simply not expecting to see him, that's all.'

Under Muller's unblinking gaze, he faltered, his nonchalance crumbling. Suddenly Barney looked every year of his age.

'Then you brought him up here, right away,' Muller continued. 'Tell me what happened then.'

For once, Parajian volubility was absent. Whether it was Hector Khassim lying murdered nearby or Olender's shaking hands Muller could not tell. But the story came slowly and reluctantly.

Mark Parajian, at his gruffest, described Khassim's arrival and withdrawal in simple, uninformative sentences.

'Now, let's get the geography straight,' Muller said, more for his own benefit than for anyone else's. 'Those offices fronting on the balcony – none of you were in them?'

There was a silent shaking of heads.

'And that office where we found Khassim was around the corner, so that it wasn't in view of the store?'

Paul Parajian bestirred himself. 'Maybe I can explain, Captain,' he said. 'Those offices on the balcony are for the benefit of the floor customers and the floor salesmen. If there's any question about delivery or payment, they can go right up those stairs without making a big circle. On the other side of the building we have the offices that handle purchasing and wholesaling, and that's where the elevator is. There is a corridor connecting the two areas on this floor.'

'And anyone could go from this part of the floor to Khassim's office without being seen from downstairs?'

Wearily Parajian nodded.

'That's what I thought,' the captain said. 'And it looks as if somebody did, doesn't it? Now, one of the secretaries says she gave Khassim a cup of coffee as soon as she got him settled. And that seems to be the only way he could have gotten the poison.' Muller thrust his head forward suddenly. 'Who knew about that cup of coffee?'

This time it was Mark Parajian who answered. 'Look, Captain, Hector was like many Middle Easterners. Whenever he was sitting at a desk, he had a cup of coffee at his elbow. And everybody in the building knew it!'

'Fine!' Muller's sarcasm was like a blast of heat. 'So any one of you could have taken some poison in there, knowing damn well there'd be something to tip it into.'

Mark shrugged. 'What do you expect me to say to that?'

'All right, let's go on from where we left off. What did you all do after Khassim left you?'

While Mark ordered his thoughts, his father took over. 'We talked for another half hour or so,' he said. 'Then our meeting broke up – '

'And Alex apparently got up and walked right out,' said Lois unexpectedly. 'Lucky Alex!'

This reinstated normalcy with a vengeance.

'I told you Alex had an appointment downtown,' Sara snapped. 'What are you trying to do?'

'Now, girls ...' Harriet pleaded desperately.

'I'm not trying to do anything,' said Lois fastidiously. 'I was simply making a comment.'

'Well, keep your comments to yourself!' Sara retorted.

Muller, however, saw his opening. 'So Mr Daniels left. That was about quarter to one? What about the rest of you? Khassim's body was discovered at one o'clock. How did the rest of you spend that fifteen minutes?'

This timetable dried up the flow again, so Muller had to do it the hard way. Direct questions elicited answers, but not much helpful information. Lois had gone to the rest room, to do her face. Paul Parajian had remained at his desk, to make that overdue call. Harriet had gone downstairs to talk to a friend in the cashier's office. Barney and Gregory had strolled back to Barney's office; then Gregory had gone in search of his wife.

'And I walked Alex out to the taxi,' said Sara, with a dirty look at her sister-in-law. 'Then I came back to see if Dad and Harriet wanted to go out for lunch. I heard the screams just as I was heading for Dad's office ...'

She bit her lip. Everybody in the room could hear Miss Martineau's ceaseless screaming again. Only Muller was unaffected. He was internally tabulating the results of this first round, and coming up with what he had expected. Anybody could have dropped in on Khassim for a minute.

When he roused himself, he found the Parajians, and Barney Olender, looking at him as if he were a dangerous animal. Perhaps it was mental telepathy that led him to ask one more question.

'While Khassim was with you, what did he say?'

In the heavy silence that followed, he knew that he had turned the tables. There was still a dangerous animal somewhere, but Captain Muller was now the hunter.

12. A Noose of Light

Gregory Parajian finally assumed the role of spokesman.

'Khassim said the trip was a sudden decision – that he had some unfinished business,' he quoted. 'Then he said he didn't want to interrupt a family discussion, so he'd wait until we were finished. That's about it, isn't it?'

His question was innocent on its face, but less perceptive men than Muller would have identified the undertone.

'You're sure that's all?' he challenged. 'Khassim didn't say anything else – like about Mrs Aratounian, for example?'

A revealing sigh was heard, but before Muller could react, Paul Parajian's no-nonsense gruffness rescued the moment.

'Hector made a joke,' he said. 'Something about maybe it was better not to be a member of this family, like poor Veron. That's all!'

This time the warning note was clear as a bell.

'Sounds like a lousy joke to me,' Muller said, watching Parajian narrowly.

There was an expressive shrug. 'Now nothing sounds right,' Parajian admitted. 'At the time, it was just a passing remark.'

'That's right,' said Gregory steadily. 'And that's all Hector said.'

By chance or design, his eyes rested on his wife.

Muller accepted the inevitable. He intended to get more information from the Parajians. But not this way.

'And we'll just have to guess,' he said softly, 'what Khassim was going to say!'

Deliberately turning away from Gregory, Lois laughed artificially. 'Well, we can't tell you that, Captain Muller!'

But Muller had already moved on. After conferring with the

patrolman at the door, he said briskly: 'All right. Now, I'm going to want to talk to each of you individually.'

Lois was not laughing now. 'You mean we can't go home?'

'Oh, no,' said Muller. 'We've still got a lot of ground to cover.'

His staff was already hard at it.

'What've we got, Arnie?' Muller asked.

By way of reply, Arnie deposited a leather briefcase on the desk, although his report began elsewhere.

'They're removing the body now,' he declared, lounging against the doorframe. 'The coffee and the rest of the samples are on their way to the lab. We've got that Martineau woman calmed down, and she's telling a pretty straight story. There was only a partition wall between her and Khassim, even though their offices opened onto different corridors. About one o'clock she heard strange noises – groans and thumps. She ran around the corner, to see Khassim writhing and clutching at the desk. Most of the stuff on the desk had been knocked to the floor. He was gasping out a few words – '

'What were they?' demanded Muller.

Arnie shook his head. 'She says it was all in some foreign language. He managed to get out the one word "poison" before he collapsed. She doesn't know whether it was a coma or whether he died right then. Anyway, he was dead by the time the doctor arrived. And nobody saw anyone going into Khassim's office. That part of the hall is never used. The front half uses the stairs, and the back half uses the elevator.'

'Dr Telfer? What does he say?' Muller asked economically.

'You know him. He's not committing himself yet. But, off the record, he's banking on cyanide. Anyway, it was something damned fast, and it wasn't nitroglycerin.'

Muller digested this. 'It figures,' he said at last. 'The killer could take a chance on the heart pills with Mrs Aratounian. Nobody suspected anything and she was feeling funny already. But Khassim? The minute his stomach started acting up, he would've been yelling for the cops. He had to be put out fast. Hell, he probably saw his murderer.'

'Not necessarily. The one witness we've got is an invoice clerk who saw Khassim in the men's room. That means the coffee was alone for a couple of minutes.'

'And a fat lot of good that does us. Either the killer went in openly and poisoned the coffee when Khassim wasn't looking, or he waited until the coast was clear. If the only witness was Khassim, he's not going to be testifying. And the Parajians all swear they were together until about quarter to one. That leaves fifteen, at most twenty, minutes ...'

'What do you make of the story the Parajians are telling?' Arnie asked curiously.

Muller smiled sourly. 'What story? They haven't told us a damned thing. All we know is that they were yakking about something – '

'The way they're yakking at each other now,' broke in a new voice. 'They want to know how much longer you're going to keep them.'

'Let them stew for a while, Harry. I want to see what else Arnie's got.'

With complacency, Arnie indicated a briefcase. 'It could be something,' he said hopefully.

Khassim's personal possessions included a dog-eared passport, a wad of traveler's checks and spare eyeglasses. There were no business papers. Whatever had brought him to New York had not required heavy documentation.

'Unless you count these,' said Arnie, who had been saving a manila envelope until the end. Turning it over, he spilled out several photographs. 'We're going to test for prints,' he said, using the sharp tip of a pencil for a pointer. 'But I thought you'd better see them first.'

Muller was already bent over in pinpoint concentration.

There were four pictures – two of them curling with age and two sepia fragments apparently cut from larger photographs. Years ago, unknown photographers had warned, 'Don't move,' and as a result, rigidly smiling, slightly cross-eyed strangers stared unseeingly into the camera and beyond.

'Who are these people?' asked Muller.

Minutes later, he was getting an answer.

'Yes,' Paul Parajian said slowly. 'They're pictures of the family. My God, that's Veron's wedding!'

The bride, slim and dusky, leaned on the shoulder of her groom. At their side a skinny young man rigidly proffered a Bible into space, his right arm pressed to his side with Prussian precision.

'And that's me,' said Parajian, puzzled.

Looking back at his younger self, he ruefully shook his head, but Muller hurried him on. He indicated the next picture, one of the fragments. The scene was again a wedding, but the entire flavor was different, the gathering larger and more informal. Here it was the groom who had his right arm clasping his wife while he offered a toast. Several of the wedding guests had survived cropping, including a young woman whose glass was being filled by a teen-aged boy.

When Parajian made no comment, Muller prodded: 'Still the family?'

'Yes, that's my wedding. My first wife and myself.'

But the explanation had come glibly enough to make the policeman suspicious. 'Never mind the couple. Who's this woman with the boy?'

'Veron,' said Parajian reluctantly. 'With my brother Haig.'

'I think we may be getting someplace.' Muller was already producing the last two photographs. 'Is she in these pictures too?'

He really had no need to ask. The same young woman was again visible, almost unchanged, as the family history continued in its natural course. It must have been a year later, because Paul Parajian was now cradling his firstborn, standing proudly next to his wife and surrounded by relatives. There was a longer gap before the final scene, which was a baptism. A priest next to the font held pride of place. Grouped around him was the family, which now included three children. Paul Parajian grasped the hand of a boy in shorts, Veron had a small girl in her charge and the teenager, now turned into a young man, held the newly christened infant.

'Must have been underexposed,' remarked Muller. 'It's awfully dark.'

'No.' Paul Parajian was lost in the past. 'Everybody's in black. Katina died giving birth to Gregory. I had almost forgotten Veron and Haig were his godparents.'

'Then it boils down to this,' Muller said remorselessly: 'Hector Khassim flew here on unexpected business, and the only thing he brought with him is four pictures of Veron Aratounian. Makes you think doesn't it?'

'God knows what Hector had in mind.'

Muller was becoming impatient. 'We can make a guess, can't we? Are you still certain it was your sister Veron who got off that plane the other day? The old lady didn't look much like this.'

'Oh, for Christ's sake!' Parajian exploded. 'You're forgetting how long it's been.' He stabbed a dramatic finger at his wedding picture. 'Does that look much like me? Hell, does that look much like Hector?'

Muller peered down at the slight figure lost among the wedding guests. 'You mean to say that's him? I wouldn't have believed it.'

But Parajian was not thinking about Hector Khassim. 'And what about the ones who died? We remember them the way they were. But Haig and Katina' – he looked down at the wife of his youth – 'they would have grown old along with the rest of us.'

Muller was deliberately matter-of-fact. 'That may be true, but it doesn't help us much.'

Parajian was still deep in his own thoughts. 'This whole thing is a nightmare.'

'Two murders? Nobody's going to quarrel with you about that,' Muller agreed. 'Now, let's start at the top again ...'

But Parajian did not add anything to Muller's fund of information.

'How could I know why Khassim came?' he repeated wearily.

'Did you think it was something serious?'

Parajian turned on his tormentor. 'Serious?' he repeated. 'God forgive me, I thought Hector was trying to worm his way in. Hector was human, you know. He was ambitious and he wanted to be more important. I assume he hurried back here because he thought he saw an opportunity.' He shook his head after this burst of frankness and added, 'Poor Hector. I'm going to miss him.'

'By "opportunity",' Muller asked quickly, 'do you mean blackmail?'

'Hector wouldn't have called it that,' Parajian replied with a faint smile.

Muller's further efforts simply confirmed what he already knew. Paul Parajian could have slipped unnoticed into Khassim's office before the body was discovered.

'I've told you what I did,' Parajian repeated. 'I called Admiral Christiansen. Then I sat and thought awhile, all alone.'

This set the pattern, and by the end of the afternoon Muller was sick of it. Any differences that emerged were those of degree. Lois Parajian, for example, was contemptuous about Khassim.

'A nasty, oily little man,' she said, wrinkling her nose in distaste. 'He was always trying to insinuate himself, one way or another.'

As for seeing Alex Daniels, she was even firmer. 'I was mistaken,' she said, without blinking an eyelash. 'I must have seen someone who looked like him. But I know now that I was mistaken.'

Gregory Parajian compulsively buttoned and unbuttoned his suit jacket, but as least he provided a change of tune.

'These old photographs? No, I've never seen them before.' he said indifferently. 'Look, while I was waiting, I got an idea. Have you considered the possibility of suicide?'

'No,' said Muller, stolidly.

'It's the only reasonable solution,' Gregory said persuasively. 'What if Hector killed Veron? That would explain why he killed himself. I think it bears looking into –'

'We will,' said Muller, speeding him on his way.

Harriet Parajian and Barney provided no surprises, but no insights either. The most uncharacteristic Parajian, however, was Mark. He kept his answers to the bare minimum.

'Yes, I saw Hector just days ago in Teheran. No, he did not speak to me about coming to New York.'

Muller let that ride for a moment, then asked, 'What did you discuss when you were over there?'

'Business,' said Mark.

'I didn't mean that,' Muller said. 'I mean, besides business. Didn't you and Khassim discuss the situation here at Parajians? Or Mrs Aratounian's murder? Or your father?'

'All we talked about,' said Mark, with the stubbornness of a bad liar, 'was business.'

From that absurd position he could not be budged, and he was no more forthcoming about the pictures. 'Sure I've seen them before. My grandmother had them on her dresser. So what?'

Sara Daniels, on the other hand, was belligerent. She did not even pretend to examine the photographs. 'Oh, I don't know. Grandmother had some wedding pictures around. But who can remember?'

'All right,' said Muller. 'Let's see what you *can* remember. Your husband left right after the meeting. That's about quarter to one, right?'

'That's right,' Sara told him. 'And I walked downstairs with him.'

She was defying him to make something of it.

'We're going to want to get a statement from him.'

'I don't see why.'

Muller's patience had its limits. 'It doesn't matter whether you see why or not, Mrs Daniels,' he said. 'I'm sending Detective Williams home with you!'

The threat went astray.

'So,' she said, rising, 'you're letting us go home – finally!'

Disgustedly, Captain Muller turned to relay further orders. 'You can tell the rest of them they can go too, Arnie.'

'Through the back door?' Arnie suggested.

'What's that?'

'Come look for yourself.'

Accompanied by Sara Daniels, Muller marched to the head of the balcony stairs. From there he could see the street.

The police cars were still there. But they had been joined by TV trucks, roving reporters and an army of cameramen. Inevitably, a huge crowd had been drawn by the prospect of excitement.

'That's why we're going to sneak everybody out the rear entrance,' Arnie explained unnecessarily. 'Not that that's going to save them for long. The Parajians have just hit the front pages.'

'Oh, my God!' said Sara Daniels, aghast.

'Yeah.' Muller was unsympathetic. It was time this bunch learned that the police were not the worst invaders of privacy.

13. My Reputation for a Song

As far as privacy was concerned, the Parajians had been living on borrowed time ever since Veron Aratounian drew her last breath. Ordinarily, the collapse of obscure elderly women in public places does not cause much excitement in newsrooms. But any overly alert reporter could have uncovered the makings of a tabloid's delight – the disputed claim to a fortune, the long-lost relative, the poisoned toast at a family reunion.

With Hector Khassim's murder, no alertness at all was required. Screaming sirens on Fifth Avenue, a retail name associated with the carriage trade and the victim's dying words spoke for themselves. The prospect of one juicy murder was enough to produce the horde outside the showroom windows. By the time several secretaries and file clerks passed through the barrage of flashbulbs, dropping incautious remarks as they went, every city-room editor knew he had a front-page story. And it came in the middle of the summer doldrums, when the rival attractions were a record attendance at Jones Beach (two and a half million cars jammed into the parking lots with no way to get out), another generator breakdown in Washington Heights (seventeen blocks without electricity for three hours) and the perennial picture of a polar bear at the Bronx Zoo, prostrate on a block of ice, looking resentful.

The radio stations were the first to trumpet the news to the world. By four o'clock it had gotten as far as Lansing, Michigan.

'The Parajians won't like this,' chortled Homer Christiansen in high fettle. He was glued to the kitchen set, drinking in every syllable. When the announcer began to speak of Veron Aratounian, he nodded wisely. 'I told you there was something fishy going on when we heard about Paul's sister. Gregory was trying to cover it up, but he didn't fool me.'

Mrs Christiansen had a talent for putting herself into other people's predicaments. She could almost hear the hail of questions, see the out-thrust microphones, feel the jostling crowd.

'Poor people!' she clucked.

Her husband flicked off the radio. 'I said they wouldn't like it, Millie,' he began ferociously. 'That doesn't mean it won't do them a lot of good.'

Roused from her nightmare of intrusive cameras and inquiring reporters, his wife stared.

'They'll get a lot of publicity for their auction. And God knows Khassim is no loss. Gregory brought him out here once, and he tried to unload some third-rate Caucasians on me.' There was a derisive bark of laughter. 'Imagine anyone telling me what will sell in Lansing!'

'Yes, yes, but I was thinking of the family, and all they'll have to go through.'

Christiansen was too single-minded for the larger sympathies. 'Do them good! They've been feeding off that business for years, and this is the first time they've had to take any knocks.'

'Well, you could say the same thing about us,' Millie reasoned as she placidly stirred the lemonade pitcher, 'and I certainly don't think a murder would do us any good.'

One of the factors in Admiral Christiansen's undistinguished naval career had been his abiding hostility to the use of reason. Civilian life gave him more latitude. Unhesitatingly he grumbled off in another direction.

'It's just like Paul's luck to have a big sale ready to roll. Come to think of it,' he continued darkly, 'I wouldn't put it past him to have stage-managed the whole thing.'

This was too much for a woman who frequently made pot roast for Paul Parajian with her own two hands.

'Homer!' she chided. 'Nobody but you would think of an auction at a time like this!'

She was wrong. At the Sotheby Parke-Bernet Galleries they made the connection like lightning.

'It's not the kind of advertising we want,' said one official austerely. 'It's a shame we've already started the mailing.'

The other's agreement was perfunctory. 'Of course. Otherwise we could have asked for a delay. Still, it's hard to say how this will affect the turnout.'

'They say that any publicity is good publicity.'

In spite of themselves, a note of cautious optimism was entering the conversation.

'We've been getting cables from all over the world asking about this auction.'

'Well, it's not surprising that the rumors have started to fly. You really ought to go downtown and take a look at those rugs. Paul Parajian has assembled the most dazzling collection of Orientals I've ever seen.'

Finally, all restraint was cast aside.

'My God! This may be the sale of the century!'

After all, even the most patrician auction galleries make their living by taking a cut off the top.

When the six-o'clock television news got its teeth into the death of Hector Khassim, Arthur Sourian was crouched over his backyard barbecue in Hempstead, trying to coax the coals into the perfect glow. His guests had all flowed into the family room to watch the film clips, and were relaying highlights through the screen door.

'Hey, Art!' they chorused. 'They're carrying the body out on a stretcher. Come and see.'

As far as Sourian was concerned, his brief glimpse of Khassim's contorted corpse had been more than enough.

'I can't leave.'

'The police are saying it's too early to tell if there's any link between this murder and the poisoning of Parajian's sister. How do you like that?'

A grunt was the only reply. Surrounded by the instruments of his calling – bellows, lighter fluid, tongs, asbestos mittens – Sourian was reaching a critical point. Already he was eyeing the pile of waiting sirloin.

But the chef's creative agony did not dampen speculation

among his guests. When the background voice began to speak of possible relief via an approaching cold front, they all surged outdoors, still chattering.

'Say, how many killings are they going to have at your place?'

'I think it's terrible the way the crime rate keeps going up –'

'Some people have all the luck. I've been with Sears for fifteen years, and the most exciting thing we've ever had is a shop-lifter.'

'Well, that can't be much of a problem at Parajians. You don't tuck a nine-by-twelve under your jacket.'

'*Wait!*' thundered Sourian. 'Phil, how do you and Marge like your steak? Rare or well done?'

'I like it rare and Marge likes it well done,' Phil replied unhelpfully. 'Now, come on, Art. Open up! You were there, after all. You must know more than that bozo on television. He just told us the basic. This Khassim was a mysterious Arab rug weaver from Baghdad who's in and out of your shop all the time. Parajian sent him to Russia to find a long-lost sister, and he brought some other dame back. Before you can say "jackrabbit" she was poisoned and then Khassim was fed the same stuff, to die in mortal agony all over a beautiful rug.'

This list of inaccuracies finally roused Sourian.

'Now, hold it. That's all wrong. Hector Khassim was a dealer from Teheran who came to New York once a year, regular as clockwork. He didn't go to Russia to find Mrs Aratounian, she found him. And finally,' he said, zeroing in on the real issue, 'Khassim died over a desk, not on one of our rugs.'

He had ticked off the points of his rebuttal with such savage precision that he effectively silenced his immediate audience. But he had no sooner picked up his long-handled fork to poke the browning meat than his wife's voice sounded.

'Art!' she yelled from the kitchen, where she was supervising a vast cauldron of boiling water and a mountain of husked corn. 'You have to tell me exactly eight minutes before you take the steaks off.'

'All right, all right,' Sourian said crossly. How, he wondered could you ask a man to barbecue steak in this cloud of distraction?

The interlude had revitalized Phil. 'You know, we saw your boss. They cornered him outside his apartment and he looked worried to death.'

'Anyone would be worried by all this bother,' Sourian answered ambiguously. 'It isn't likely ...' He broke off, galvanized into action. 'Corn!' he bellowed, seizing his fork and advancing on the grill like a picador stalking the bull.

The next few minutes were a maelstrom of activity. Eddies of steam rose from the kitchen window, a gigantic bowl of salad and a platter of garlic bread appeared on the table, a carafe of wine was handed from glass to glass. Through it all, Arthur Sourian prodded and flipped, muttering cabalistically to himself: 'Three well dones, five rares, two mediums.'

By the time he had shoveled the last steak onto the last plate, he was a mellowed man. 'You know,' he said as though launching an entirely new subject, 'this is the worst possible time for Khassim to get murdered. I'm not saying it wouldn't have meant trouble whenever it happened, but by now it's no secret that the Parajians are doing some infighting. Mr Parajian has gambled his whole reputation on this big auction that's coming up. And I mean big! Even the insurance people are impressed. They're demanding special guards and all sorts of extra precautions. We're all working overtime. Just preparing the catalog has been a major job, and it's an art object in itself. Mark has been shuttling up to the gallery to fight about the hanging and lighting for the preview, Gregory's got every dealer in this country hopping with excitement and I hate to think what our overseas phone bill is.'

'What does that have to do with this poisoning?' asked Marge, buttering cobs steadily.

'Don't you see? Mr Parajian was betting that he still knows the rug market, and this sale would prove it. But the whole auction could be torpedoed by something that has nothing to do with the market, and then where will he be? The last thing in the world he needs right now is a front-page murder. It's making plenty of problems for him.'

The murder of Hector Khassim was making problems for

other people, as well. The eleven-o'clock news had barely finished before Ken Nicolls' phone was ringing. The call was from Truro, Massachusetts.

'Jane!' he said, alarmed. 'Is everything all right with you and the children?'

'Of course. But I just saw you on television, coming away from that murder. They said you were there when he died. It must have been awful.'

'I was in the same building, that's all. He didn't die at my feet, or anything like that.'

Reassured, Jane turned to more wifely subjects. 'What were you doing in Parajians anyway?'

This was exactly the question Ken hoped she would not ask. Almost without thinking, he said: 'I was there for the Sloan. You remember, I told you we're handling the Parajian trust.'

Some deep instinct told him to produce a rug, *then* discuss its price.

'Of course, I should have realized. But good heavens, Ken, when we talked there'd been only one murder and you said the Parajians were already hysterical. They must be wild now.'

Some Parajians had other things to think about. By mid-morning the Sunday *Times*, with over twenty columns of fine print about murders, the Middle East and rugs, had made its way to Amagansett, Long Island.

Corinne Parajian had not disturbed a single one of its folds. She was studying Mexican road maps with her fiancé.

'So right after the wedding we fly to El Paso, where we pick up the camper. You're sure it will be ready for us, Bud?'

'Absolutely. But I'll call the day before to double-check. We have two weeks to fool around Mexico City and Acapulco and Guadalajara. Then we head for the bush and we're on our own,' he said eagerly.

Corinne wrinkled her nose in doubt. 'What about supplies? You remember what happened in Maine?'

'But this is a camper!' Maine had made an indelible impression on both of them. Even young love can go just so far on a box of soggy saltines. 'If we pack it right, I figure we can be independent of stores for a week at a time.'

'Good. Then all we have to take is our clothes.'

'And that new movie camera your father is lending us. I was going to ask him to show me how it works this morning, but I haven't seen him around.'

'Oh, I wouldn't ask him today.' Corinne had adopted the voice she used to deal with the generation gap. 'Have you seen the headlines?'

Bud was totally uninterested. 'Sure. What's that got to do with it?'

'Well, you know how hung up he is on respectability. That murder down at the store has really gotten to him. This morning he came down, had one look around and took off. I think the strain is beginning to tell.'

Mark Parajian had put it even more strongly when he rousted his father from the breakfast table to go fishing. He was, he said, pretty damned fed up.

Father and son were reclining in the stern of the boat, idly trolling. Mark was wearing Amagansett's fishing costume – a polo shirt, drip-dry pants and a long-billed cap. But Paul belonged to an older school of anglers. His dungarees, so worn and faded that they were the envy of every passing teen-ager, and his shabby gray sweatshirt were bad enough. But crowning the whole was an ancient panama. Originally it had formed part of the summer uniform demanded of city merchants. For years now it had been fishing gear. Its natural ventilation was augmented with the broken holes left by hooks and flies, its ribbon was eroded to a tattered string, its brim drooped in irregular waves. At the moment it was tilted forward to rest on its owner's nose.

'Things pretty bad at your house?' Paul Parajian asked finally.

'Unbelievable.' But two hours of spanking sea breezes had blown most of Mark's ill-humor away. He was stirred to a fluency that would have surprised Captain Muller. 'The wedding presents were supposed to go on the ping-pong table in the rec room. And that's where they started. But somehow they've taken over the whole first floor. You find the strangest things in the strangest places. This morning I found a check from the Stewarts under the toaster.'

Paul's grunt was enough to keep Mark going. 'At the beginning of all this, Helen and Corinne said she wasn't going to need a trousseau. Well, I don't know what they call what she's got, but the second floor is knee-deep in boxes and tissue paper and wrappings.'

'What's in the boxes?' Paul asked, evincing mild curiosity.

'There seem to be about a hundred bathing suits and a hundred pairs of sandals. Nothing else.'

'She'd do better to get some insect repellent and some mosquito netting for this famous honeymoon of theirs.' Paul was not enthusiastic about starting married life in the bush.

This reminded Mark of another irritant. 'They say it's not a honeymoon because they've been living with each other for a year.'

'Wait until they find out they're stuck with each other.'

Mark grinned. 'They don't think that makes any difference.'

'Well, all you have to do is get through the next two weeks and Corinne's wedding will be behind you.'

'So will your auction.' Mark's spirits had been rising. 'But I'll say one thing for your auction, at least it's not taking place under my roof.'

'Why do you think people are willing to give auctioneers a percentage?' Paul asked lazily. Then, removing his hat and squinting at the sun, he became aware of a need. 'You wouldn't be heading for the beer cooler, would you?'

When Mark returned, he held a dripping bottle against his cheek and confided: 'Sometimes I think life must have been a lot simpler, being poor in Greece. I'll bet your wedding wasn't like this.'

'My wedding!' Paul stared, then hooted. 'By now you should know that the groom doesn't count. I don't remember much about my wedding, but I'll never forget Veron's. Poor people go through the same motions as rich people, but they do it much less comfortably. Everything that's going on in your ten-room split-level was crowded into our two rooms. Maybe more. I seem to remember a lot of sewing.'

Even mention of Veron could not cloud this cloudless day. Mark leaned back luxuriously and waxed philosophic: 'Only two weeks more and everything will be behind us.'

Paul Parajian did not think he was talking about weddings and auctions.

14. Like Foolish Prophets

By lunchtime on Monday, John Thatcher had already added the testimony of an eyewitness to the effusions of the media.

'Not that Nicolls was able to tell me much. He saw Khassim's actual arrival and how it affected Barney Olender. But that doesn't do much good,' he reported.

He was in a taxicab with Charlie Trinkam and Walter Bowman, the Sloan's chief of research. They were returning from a Security Analysts' luncheon, and even murder was a pleasanter topic than the current market outlook.

'You know, Ev asked me to keep my ear to the ground for anything I could pick up about the Parajians,' Bowman began.

His two companions looked at him respectfully. The Bowman ear was famous the length of Wall Street. Over the years it had produced one gilt-edged opportunity after another, while at the same time keeping the Sloan from getting burned. These days, only God Almighty could prevent a little singeing.

'Well, now,' said Charlie happily, 'that means you know everything worth knowing about them.'

'No, it doesn't. Parajians is a closely held corporation, and nobody outside the IRS has ever seen their accounts. Oh, they've done plenty of borrowing over the years, but it's always been commercial loans secured by inventory. The one thing everybody knows is that they keep one hell of an inventory. Paul Parajian's got quite a reputation. He's always taken big chances on which way rugs will go, and he's always been right.'

Thatcher nodded. 'That's the risk-taking his children are alarmed about. But I was hoping for something more definitive about the company. We've heard talk about Parajian stock in connection with control. But how much money is it worth?'

'It's the same old textbook case,' Charlie weighed in. 'As long as there's no market for a stock, you can't price it. Not until a buyer makes an offer.'

Walter Bowman was triumphant. 'I said I didn't have any numbers for you, but I do have a fact. They're not making any noise about it, but for the past couple of years United Department Stores has been wanting to acquire Parajians. The rumor is that they'd give their eyeteeth for it.'

'Ah ha!' Pure intellectual satisfaction was exercising Thatcher. 'There's your price, Charlie. United must have made several offers and every member of the Parajian family knows it.'

'Okay, Walter,' Charlie said. 'Spill it! Which Parajian needs money?'

Neither Thatcher nor Trinkam ever doubted that Bowman could tell them.

'None of them is exactly down to his last shekel. Paul Parajian takes a lot out of the company and lives pretty high, but nothing out of reason. He's got an apartment in town and a summer place in Amagansett. Mark lives year round in Amagansett, and stays well within his income. Apparently the two families see a lot of each other.'

Charlie brushed aside this financial virtue. 'What about the others? Anything there?'

'Gregory has one of those fancy cooperative apartments, lives the big-city life and consistently overspends. But it's the daughter who's interesting. She and her husband have a business of their own that's within an inch of bankruptcy.'

'No wonder she was trying to get an advance from Everett,' Thatcher remarked. 'What kind of business is it?'

'They make those small greenhouses.'

'What?' For a moment Charlie Trinkam balked. A lifelong bachelor, he was unprepared for certain aspects of American suburban life. But he recovered quickly. 'Well, there you have it. The two of them are hipped on their business, and suddenly it needs cash. They decide to oust Paul Parajian, sell their stock and pick up an extra slice from their aunt's death as a bonus.'

Bowman did not have the imaginative fire of his colleague. 'That's not exactly the way the script runs,' he protested.

'These greenhouses have been in the red all along. And every time there's a real emergency, Daddy comes to the rescue.'

'Mrs Daniels didn't look like a desperate woman when she applied to Everett,' Thatcher corroborated. 'It seemed to be a *pro forma* gesture, before she did what she knew she was going to do all along.'

'Great!' Charlie said sarcastically. 'Walter's proved that none of the Parajians had to get up to any fancy tricks.'

'A simple need for money would scarcely explain the murders of Mrs Aratounian and Hector Khassim, anyway. But you don't have to look far for complications. At one time Everett was deeply suspicious of Khassim's role with Mrs Aratounian.'

Charlie could spot holes too. 'Khassim might have produced a ringer to get hold of that fifteen percent. But murdering her wouldn't do any good. And now he's been murdered, himself.'

'I thought Ev had something else up his sleeve,' said Bowman, who had been too busy with the prime rate to keep abreast of Gabler's misgivings.

'That was when he learned about the children. Parajian lost sight of them during the war,' Thatcher explained, 'and then Khassim found them in a DP camp. I gather they were accepted, more or less, on their own word.'

Bowman whistled, and Charlie burst into speech. 'What a setup!' he marveled. 'If Khassim was hot to worm his way into the business, that was the way to do it.'

'You're going too fast, Charlie. First of all, this happened in 1948, before Parajians expanded into a million-dollar business. Second, nobody could predict that Paul Parajian would be so generous with his gifts of stock. Third, Veron Aratounian could scarcely have been a threat. She hadn't seen the children since they were infants.'

Charlie tried knocking down the objections, one by one:

'In 1948, every middle-class American businessman looked like a millionaire to people who'd just been through a war. Maybe Khassim was farsighted. And it was a cinch that Parajian would take the kids into the business. You don't have to own stock to milk a company. If Khassim was a supplier and one of the kids was a buyer, there would be plenty of room for hanky-panky. As far as Veron goes, you can't tell with women,' Charlie said largely. 'Maybe she remembered scars from some accident or the fact that they'd never had the measles.'

'You're making it all too tricky,' argued Bowman. 'Look, there's a lot of money sitting in the Aratounian trust waiting for somebody to pick it up. Right?'

'Subject to certain safeguards,' murmured Thatcher, who did not like this cavalier description of his department's methods.

'Yeah, yeah. Then an old lady comes out of the blue, claims to be Mrs Aratounian and is knocked off before her brother can ask any inconvenient questions. The net result is that her estate is going to be distributed to the very people who were yelling for more leverage in the company. I say one of them was the producer of this scenario.'

'And Khassim?' Charlie asked skeptically.

'He tumbled to it and came rushing back, either to tell all or to blackmail somebody.'

'Then why the delay? I know the mysterious East has different ideas about time than we do. But if Khassim saw someone tip the poison into the old lady's drink, why a round trip of ten thousand miles before he does something about it?'

No one, thought Thatcher, could maintain that a career in banking stunted the spirit of invention. If anything, it seemed to stimulate the faculty. He tried to measure up to his subordinates.

'I doubt if Khassim spotted the poisoning itself. You're right, Charlie, anything that cut-and-dried would have evoked a response from him before he went back to Iran. But Walter may still have a point. There is one area where an impersonation could have gone astray.'

Bowman simply cocked his head receptively.

'It was to Paul Parajian's advantage to rush Mrs Aratounian over here, as soon as she showed up in Khassim's office. The murderer might have been relying on that. Instead, Parajian bent over backwards to ensure that his sister's health, rather than his own self-interest, took first priority. The result was an unexpected stay in Teheran of several weeks, with Khassim seeing the woman regularly.'

'But Khassim wasn't an old friend of Veron's,' said Bowman, unconvinced. 'He himself said that he'd only seen her once or twice about forty years ago. How well do you get to know the bride at a wedding? Most of the ones I've seen I wouldn't recognize on the street a month later.'

Thatcher expanded: 'The danger wasn't that Khassim knew Veron, the danger was that Khassim knew Paul in the old days. Obviously his suspicions weren't roused at once. But back home, he might have remembered some curious mistake by the new Veron. He might even have been told something by his granddaughter who had seen a lot of Mrs Aratounian.'

'Once you start thinking in that direction,' said Charlie reflectively, 'it could be anything.'

'For Christ's sake, it's still forty years. People forget things.' Walter Bowman might have amplified his dogmatism, but he was attacked on his flank.

'Don't you believe it!'

Everybody had overlooked the cabby. But he had been following the conversation with growing interest.

'I don't know anything about that murder in the rug store,' he declared, 'but I can tell you one thing. I've got an older sister on the Coast I haven't seen for ten years, but she could give you chapter and verse about every time I had poison ivy, how I acted at my high school graduation and who the first girl I dated was.'

Stunned by this intervention, Bowman confessed that he himself did not have a sister.

'I thought so!' the cabby said coolly. 'Well, take it from me, anybody pretending to be my sister Gladys would have to stay clear of my cousins, my old neighbors, my old teachers and my old truant officer.'

Thatcher used the raw material he had been given. 'That's interesting. What you're saying is, it's the old contacts who could expose an impostor, not the new ones. A false Veron Aratounian could deceive almost anybody but Hector Khassim. Always excluding Paul Parajian.'

'And the murderer didn't give her enough time to run into

trouble with Parajian. All right, I'll give you that.' Bowman was not risking any more generalities about old family memories. 'That means the plan called for her to be killed.'

'Stop right there!' commanded Charlie Trinkam. 'You're talking about a pretty dumb old lady who agrees to a plan like that.'

Now they were on Bowman's territory. 'Remember Home-Stake Production Company? You wave enough profit at people and they don't see what the logical end is.'

He had, of course, just explained the success of every major swindle since the first sale of choice, waterfront lots on Mount Ararat.

'This is pure theory,' Thatcher mused, 'and not susceptible to proof, unless Khassim confided in someone.'

'Did Nicolls say how Khassim explained his sudden return?' asked Bowman.

'Apparently he simply gave an enigmatic smile and announced that he had discovered some unfinished business. But Nicolls did extract some general information from the sales force. Khassim's visits to New York were always scheduled well in advance. The whole purpose was to keep him up to date about the American market, so Gregory laid on a whole agenda of appointments with major outlets.'

'Then Gregory was the one Khassim would deal with?'

Thatcher could see where Trinkam was heading. 'There seems to be a functional division of work at Parajians. Gregory takes care of the wholesaling in this country. Paul runs the retail stores from New York to Honolulu. And Mark ...'

'Yes?' asked Bowman at this significant pause.

'Mark does the buying in the Near East.'

'It doesn't take much to read between those lines,' said Charlie, his buoyancy restored. 'Are you saying that Mark is the only one who trots around that part of the world?'

'Paul used to. He's given it up in the past few years.'

'So if any Parajian wanted to locate an old Armenian lady with some knowledge of Russia and no knowledge of America, Mark stands out like a sore thumb.'

'It sounds almost too logical,' said Thatcher as the taxi finally bullied its way through the last tie-up to arrive at the Sloan.

By the time they were in the elevator, Charlie had absorbed this remark and drawn his own inference.

'Logic does seem out of place with this bevy of beauties,' he conceded. 'If anybody did coach a ringer, it will probably turn out to be the American wife, the sweetie-pie who sends Everett up the wall.'

'That was in the old days,' Thatcher corrected him. 'I'll say one thing for these murders. They've shifted the wall-climbing away from the Sloan.'

How wrong he was he learned the moment he set foot in his own suite of offices. Every secretary in the trust department was there, except his own.

'Where is Miss Corsa?' he demanded. 'And what's going on?'

The result was like directing a glee club to let loose without specifying the selection.

'Miss Todd took her away . . .'

'The police are here!'

' . . . Mr Gabler called a lawyer.'

And finally, loud and clear:

'They're going to arrest Mr Nicolls!'

While Thatcher goggled, trying to dredge some rationality from these demented sentences, he saw, with immeasurable relief, the approaching figure of the only person capable of taming this whirlwind. Confidently he waited to see melodrama dispelled, fear allayed and normalcy restored.

Instead his Miss Corsa, who never dictated to him in the presence of hourly personnel, said tightly:

'Mr Thatcher, you had better go to Mr Nicolls' office immediately.'

15. One Luckless Human Soul

In spite of what Kipling says, when two strong men stand face to face there is likely to be a collision. Within seconds of arriving at the scene of combat, Thatcher realized that Ken Nicolls was in danger of being flattened by the impact.

Captain Muller and Everett Gabler were both on their toes, with jaws outthrust, well past the point of no return. There the similarity ended. Muller wanted to arrest Ken Nicolls; Gabler wanted to fire him.

The barrage of recriminations and threats soon told Thatcher what had happened. Captain Muller, reviewing the list of witnesses at Parajians, had discovered the existence of a Sloan spy on the premises. He had raced up from Centre Street, cornered Ken Nicolls and demanded details of his mission. Confronted with a blanket denial, Muller had been ready to erupt when Everett appeared.

'If you think you can get away with an end run around the police, you've got another think coming. I was promised co-operation from you. Instead, you come up with something and send this guy nosing into Parajians. Well, let me tell you, I can have him in the can so fast for obstruction – '

Everett, unfortunately absent this morning during Nicolls' debriefing, had just come across a familiar name in the morning paper. Knowing that no legitimate bank business called for Nicolls' visit to Parajians, Gabler had stalked down the corridor. He discovered his subordinate closeted with Muller, delivering a clandestine report.

'The Sloan will not tolerate the use of its personnel as under-cover auxiliaries. The city employs men for precisely that purpose. If you want someone to masquerade as a rug customer, use one of your own people. As far as Nicolls is concerned, if his loyalties are divided, he can go!'

Unfortunately, in Thatcher's view, there could be no doubt that Muller and Gabler were both passionately attached to their respective organizations. Rather than countenance a subversion of police methods, Captain Muller would throw the entire population of New York City into jail. And Everett was quite ready to run the Sloan single-handed sooner than suffer one mote of imperfection in its roster of employees.

So far all was clear. Under the circumstances, it would not have been astonishing to find Nicolls cowering behind his desk in abject terror. But why was the boy the picture of confused guilt?

Thatcher could not know that Ken was tangled in the web of his own duplicity. At all times he had to remember that his story to Jane was that he had gone to Fifth Avenue as an emissary of the Sloan, and that his story to Muller was that he had gone on his own. The life of a double agent is never easy.

'One moment, please!' bellowed Thatcher, taking a calculated risk. 'Captain Muller, you say you have a list of customers in the store when Khassim was murdered?'

By this time Muller knew that you have to watch everyone at the Sloan like a hawk. 'Yes,' he admitted warily. 'That's how I found out about this joker.'

'And how many other bankers were there?'

Thatcher knew his finesse had paid off before Muller said a word. The captain's double take, the defensive hunching of his shoulders, was answer enough. And the risk had not been that great. Young Nicolls had been at the Sloan long enough to start adopting some tribal customs.

'All right. I see what you're driving at,' said Muller. 'As a matter of fact, there was a vice president from the Morgan Guaranty and a guy called Dornhoff from the Second National City.'

'Dornhoff?' Gabler's professional instincts were roused. 'How much was he spending?'

'How the hell should I know?' Honest to God, Muller thought, these bankers came up with questions no cop would dare ask.

Thatcher intervened hurriedly. 'Now, Captain, if two other banks have men innocently occupied at Parajians, there is nothing implausible about Nicolls' being there for the same reason.'

Muller might be temporarily baffled by the domestic habits of the financial community, but Gabler was right in his element. 'If Nicolls' actions are blameless, why has he been concealing them? If I had not happened to read the account in the *Times* with great care – '

But Thatcher waved him to a halt. 'No, Everett. Nicolls was in my office first thing this morning. We tried to find you' – here he became heavily reproachful – 'but your secretary didn't know where you were.'

Now, there was no greater foe of the unscheduled absence from the Sloan than Everett. More than one lunch hour in the executive dining room had passed in measured diatribe against luminaries from International and Investment who were not at their desks when needed. And Gabler's practice was almost as good as his preaching. His lapses over the past thirty years could be counted on one hand.

Knowing full well that it was a tactical error, he rushed into self-exculpation. 'I stopped by the Soviet office to pick up some papers about Mrs Aratounian. It took much longer than I anticipated.'

He had just waved a red flag.

'That's another thing,' Muller said, rearing up. 'Our understanding was that you were going to let me know what you found out. And not a word have I heard from you.'

'Well, you're hearing one now. The woman who died in our foyer was Mrs Veron Aratounian, just as she claimed.'

'Yeah? And what little bird gave you that tip?'

Gabler smiled thinly. 'My informants wouldn't interest you, Captain. But I can assure you that the Sloan is now willing to accept Mrs Aratounian's identity.'

Thatcher was beginning to wish that he had told Miss Corsa to mind her own business. The Sloan could struggle along without Ken Nicolls. Losing Gabler would cause a major upheaval. And Everett was displaying all the symptoms of a man eager to follow countless reporters into the nearest cell, to protect his sources.

But it was a mistake to underestimate Captain Muller. In a display of perception that would have amazed the American Psychiatric Association, he shrugged lightly. 'Well, it's a fine theory,' he said. 'But just because you think the old lady was Mrs Aratounian doesn't mean we're any further.'

'Theory! Think!' Everett could not believe his ears. 'I told you we are now ready to wind up the trust.'

'Look, I don't know how you run your bank, Mr Gabler,' answered Muller, feeding the flames, 'but a murder investigation is a serious business. We have to operate on hard evidence.'

'And what do you imagine the Sloan requires?' Everett was already slamming down the red accordion envelope he had been carrying. 'Perhaps you will take the time to glance through these.'

Thatcher felt like applauding Muller's performance, but considered it wiser to confine himself to drawing up a chair.

As Gabler wrestled with the string, he relapsed into his normal didactic tones. 'There was no problem in documenting Mrs Aratounian's early life. Indeed, we have more material than I expected.'

The first fistful of papers, each with an English translation attached, supported this statement. There was an early census listing Harum Aratounian, living with his wife, Veron, in a small town near Delizhan. There were employment records for Harum in Yerevan. A casualty list from World War II included the Aratounian son. Then came the death of Harum.

'Now we have the exit papers,' Gabler continued, releasing a second sheaf. 'You will see that her departure from Russia was legal and orderly.'

The application for an emigration visa cited the loss of all relatives in the Soviet Union. The existence of both family and funds in the United States was claimed on the appropriate line. Stapled to the approval of this application was a signed waiver of pension rights. Finally, there was an affidavit from the emigration officer who had handled the case. Clearance had been delayed while he questioned Mrs Aratounian's method of departure. If the brother and the money were in New York, then the sensible course was a flight to New York. But Mrs Aratounian had been adamant, She preferred to go to Teheran. As her health and her funds were adequate for the trip, the officer had ultimately yielded.

A puzzled frown appeared on Muller's face. 'If this is true, why did she have to be rushed to a nursing home in Iran?'

Gabler was still reserving a folder. 'That took a certain amount of investigation. But the Soviet Union has been surprisingly co-operative, and it appears that they have a good many sources in that area of the world.'

John Thatcher was growing impatient. 'Yes, yes, Everett. The press reminds us of that every time there's a flare-up in the Middle East.'

Unperturbed, Gabler swept on. With fingertip to fingertip, he was the model of prudence. 'On the whole, I am inclined to accept their information as accurate.'

No higher accolade would ever be bestowed on the KGB, thought Thatcher.

'Splendid,' he said. 'What have you got?'

Barely able to contain his triumph, Everett slid onto the table a photostat of a police report filed in an Iranian border town a week before Mrs Aratounian's dramatic descent on the offices of Hector Khassim. When Muller saw the heading on the translation, his eyebrows crawled right up into his hairline.

'Jesus Christ,' he muttered, 'I wonder what they've got from *my* files.'

According to Police Officer Joumi, a foreign national, one Veron Gregorievna Aratounian, had lodged a complaint about purse-snatching. The sum allegedly stolen was so large that Officer Joumi had tried to help Mrs Aratounian. He had proposed calling the Soviet Embassy, the American Embassy or the offices of Khassim Enterprises. Mrs Aratounian had rejected all suggestions, maintaining that her suitcase contained her passport and enough cash for her journey.

'Both the emigration officer and Joumi end their reports on the same plaintive note,' Thatcher remarked.

'She must have been one hell of a stubborn old lady,' said

Muller, answering the spirit of the comment. 'She'd made up her mind exactly where and how she was contacting her brother, and nobody was going to persuade her to do it any other way. But it's easy enough to figure what happened. Instead of a short, first-class flight to Teheran, she only had the money for third-class buses or trains or whatever they have there. It took a lot longer, and she didn't have enough to eat regularly. She ended up in a state of collapse.'

'But still clutching her passport.' Everett shared Mrs Aratounian's gift for ending up where he wanted.

'I grant you it proves she was the genuine article. It's too bad,' Muller complained. 'I had a nice theory about Khassim tumbling to one of her mistakes.'

Thatcher was mindful of his taxi ride. 'Who did not?' he murmured. 'Now we'll have to concentrate on Khassim.'

'And good luck to us,' the policeman said irritably. 'Khassim sure as hell tumbled to something. He didn't come shooting back to New York just for the ride.'

Thanks to Gabler's endeavors, the Sloan now had enough credit to ask a few questions of its own. 'I suppose there is no clue to what that might be,' Thatcher fished.

'Nothing more than a general tone.' Muller sounded disgusted. 'See what you make of it. Khassim strolls into the place, saying in a mysterious voice that he has unfinished business. Well, you met him. Five to one, a mysterious voice was one of his specialties. Then he finds all the Parajians together, so he drops a couple of remarks about how they're not such good friends as they thought, and how Veron would still be alive if she hadn't gotten too close to her family. What does that boil down to? If Khassim was about to put the bite on someone, it stands to reason that things were going to get a little unfriendly. And we already know that Veron made a big mistake drinking anything under the Parajian roof.'

'Remarkably unhelpful,' Thatcher sympathized. 'And I suppose he didn't get a chance to say anything more.'

'Not in words. But in his briefcase, he was carrying these pictures.' Muller fanned them out on the desk top. 'You see why I was disappointed with what Mr Gabler told us. Four pictures of the real Veron Aratounian seemed to be a pointer.'

Everett did not even bother to examine the woman whose past he had researched so indefatigably. 'We can dispense with that supposition,' he said loftily.

'Of course, in the meantime, another screwy item has turned up,' Muller went on, testing the water. 'I didn't realize that the Parajian kids had been missing persons all through the war. It makes you think, doesn't it?'

'We ourselves were only informed of that circumstance the other day,' Gabler replied. 'I agree that it is unusual.'

In some indefinable way, Muller was disappointed with this response. He fell back on a ploy that had already proved its worth.

'But having a lot of bright ideas isn't much help. No one could miss noticing that Khassim was the one who found the kids. They owe him a lot. Whether or not they paid off is anybody's guess.'

'While investigating Mrs Aratounian's *bona fides*, I felt it my duty to have our banking associates in Iran look into Khassim's affairs. He received no money directly from any Parajian, except as payment for rugs.'

Muller could recognize code words. 'Directly?' he repeated to himself. 'So unless you could check up on this end, you'd never know, would you?'

They were on very tricky ground indeed.

'It just so happens,' said Everett, looking impossibly virtuous, 'my inquiries reveal that no money has flowed out of the country from any Parajian personal account.'

'It just so happens, does it?' echoed Thatcher.

Everett hurried into speech. 'This simply proves again that doing a job well in the first place is always an economy in the long run. The Sloan will not have to embark on any new – and costly – searches. In the course of validating Mrs Aratounian, we have necessarily explored the background of the Parajian children, at least insofar as possible.'

Muller might be confused by Gabler's justification, but he was making hay while the sun shone.

'I suppose you couldn't find out anything,' he asked ingenuously.

Unfortunately, Everett Gabler was not a miracle worker. He had reams of material on the children before the war and after 1948, but no connective tissue.

'It was too much to hope for,' Muller admitted. 'We'll never know whether this is just some crazy idea springing up because of the Aratounian mess.'

Until now Ken Nicolls had been too shell-shocked to draw attention to himself. But as his elders spoke, he had been studying Khassim's faded photographs.

'But there's one indicator, isn't there? This baptism picture, it's got all three kids in it. Khassim must have picked it out specially.'

'I've been over that thing with a microscope,' Muller grunted. 'I'm not saying there isn't something there. Maybe there's a vaccination or something I'm missing. But you'd have to be a member of that family to spot it, and they're not giving anything away. They're just sitting back, waiting to collect their inheritance.'

This observation reacted unfavorably on Everett, and worse was still to come. Captain Muller was punctilious about expressing his indebtedness to the Sloan. 'You've saved us a lot of time, Mr Gabler,' he said. 'God knows how long it would have taken us to come up with anything as comprehensive as this.'

Momentarily Everett was struck dumb to hear it suggested that any agency on earth could rival the Sloan's prodigies of effort.

'We're always happy to cooperate,' said Thatcher, taking over the niceties of leave-taking. 'Although I'm afraid all we've provided is some confirmation.'

'Don't knock it,' Muller told him. 'The more underbrush we clear away, the sooner we'll see what's left.'

16. A Voice Within the Tavern

Once, in the misty dawn of time, the U.S. Post Office had lost an important communication from the trust department of the Sloan. As a result, Everett Gabler turned against first-class mail; nowadays, even routine requests for Social Security numbers were festooned with costly precautions. Lacking federal marshals riding shotgun, Gabler had experimented with Special Handling, Certified Mail and Insurance, then finally settled on Registered, Return Receipt Requested. The torrent of green-paper scraps pouring into his office made Mrs Norris swear under her breath, but provided Everett with the only confidence this uncertain world affords.

So in short order, Gabler learned that Mrs Aratounian's heirs had each received the Sloan's verification of her identity. Simultaneously, however, he learned about a technical snag encountered by Vitamedical, Inc. Given Everett, disposable thermometers immediately displaced the Parajians.

'Vitamedical has consistently botched its excellent opportunities through sheer incompetence,' he sputtered to John Thatcher as they left the investment committee.

Walter Bowman was the Sloan expert on casualties among promising firms with high hopes. 'That's the trouble with bright prospects,' he contributed. 'People get blinded by the glare.'

'I personally advised them to defer this second factory until they signed the contract with Johnson and Johnson.' Everett, denouncing sin, was a hard man to stop.

'Look at Cassandra,' Walter replied comfortably. He had not recommended Vitamedical.

'Sensible advice can scarcely be construed as a prophecy of woe!'

'Try telling that to the Greeks!' Walter countered.

For the sake of peace, as well as accuracy, Thatcher said, 'Trojans, I believe, Walter.'

'Trojans, Greeks or Zulus!' Walter philosophized. 'They're all the same!'

He could well have added Armenians.

'... I like this layout! Or that other one. Where was the format I threw away earlier?'

Paul Parajian, shirt sleeves rolled up, pawed bearlike through the papers and sketches piled high on his desk.

'Here it is!' cried a young man, swooping to retrieve a folder from under Parajian's heel. 'This is the one we recommend.'

'I'll look it over again.' Parajian snatched at it. 'Mmm ...'

'It's simple and dignified – and it coordinates with the catalog and the invitations,' the young man coaxed, while a female assistant behind him nodded fervently. On the couch, a sharp-featured woman with a vivid gray streak in her hair blew a fat smoke ring.

'Let me think about it some more,' Parajian rumbled.

The trio from Cosmo Medici Graphic Consultants honored this request, even when the door opened to admit Barney Olender and Harriet.

'I still think we should list some of our best rugs,' Parajian said finally. 'Or just mention the Ushak – '

The heaviest gun at Cosmo Medici was the chain-smoking Miss Mintz. 'The auction list and the catalog are available to serious customers,' she said, opening a portfolio and pointing. 'They've got all the details, including our photographs, which are real knockouts. For the public announcement, which is just a formality, in the newspapers and weeklies ...'

Mention of newspapers was enough to make Harriet Parajian shudder and glance at Barney. Paul, noticing her arrival for the first time, said, 'What do you think, Harriet?'

'What do I think about what?'

'Just mentioning some of the rugs we want to sell,' he said with heavy irony aimed at the couch.

He was enjoying himself, but only Harriet could tell.

Barney barely got out his comment – 'Maybe you're right about that, Paul' – before Miss Mintz took over.

'Lists of rugs with prices are fine for quickie sales in motels,' she said superciliously. 'But when Parajians holds an auction at Parke-Bernet, we're in a different league. A very simple, very dignified announcement is the only way to do it.'

Harriet was reminded of Corinne's wedding counselor, until Miss Mintz added: 'And we've got to offset the other publicity Parajians has been getting lately.'

Paul looked like thunder, while Cosmo Medici quivered. Miss Mintz simply blew another lazy smoke ring past Barney and said: 'We've got beautiful catalogs. We've got great invitations. It would be a shame to spoil it all with a shlocky public announcement.'

This tipped the balance. 'Okay,' Paul Parajian capitulated with a histrionic shrug. 'You're the pros. You know best – '

'That's right!' said Miss Mintz, nearly spoiling the moment.

The departure of Cosmo Medici Graphic Consultants came none too soon.

'My God!' said Paul, when Cosmo finally trailed off in Miss Mintz's wake. 'The Parke-Bernet people are bringing the auctioneer over this afternoon, too. And I used to think medical specialists were bad! If I'd known then what I know now, I never would have touched this auction.'

Harriet did not need Barney's conspiratorial nudge. 'I wish you meant that, Paul,' she said in a rush.

Suddenly wary, he retreated to his desk. 'I never asked what brought you – both of you – here.'

Barney knew what chivalry required. 'Paul,' he said manfully, 'Harriet dropped by today, and we got talking. That is, I just happened to mention how I feel – and Harriet says she agrees. Or at least thinks – '

It was not the first time Harriet had watched Paul's amusement when Barney sank into a quagmire of his own making. Today she was too worried to be appreciative.

She broke in: 'Is it too late to postpone the auction?'

'Has Mark been talking to you? Or maybe Sara? Gregory doesn't object – or at least, I thought so. Of course, I could be wrong. I've been too busy to keep up with the latest developments.' Paul was suddenly intent. 'They've all heard from the Sloan, haven't they? Do they think that means that they're going to be able to take over right away? Or have they – ?'

'Paul!' To her horror, Harriet heard tears in her voice.

Barney was appalled. 'You're barking up the wrong tree, Paul,' he hastened to say. 'Harriet and I haven't been putting our heads together with the kids. You should know better. Besides, I think they're all willing to go along with the auction. I don't say they're crazy about it. But they're not fighting it.'

It was not in Parajian's nature to apologize. 'Then, what's this talk about postponing?'

By now, Harriet was composed enough to spell Barney. 'You know as well as we do,' she declared. 'Ever since Hector's murder, it's been undiluted hell. Oh, you don't mind, Paul, and I can endure it. But it's not easy on the others. No, I am not talking about Lois and her complaints! I'm talking about Helen and Corinne. Yes, and Mark and Gregory too. Wouldn't it be better to let some time pass? Wouldn't it be better to have the great Parajian auction at Parke-Bernet sometime later?'

Barney remembered that he was a hard-nosed businessman. 'Oh, sure, it would cost something. You'd be carrying inventory for a couple of months, not to speak of the catalog and everything – '

'No!' said Parajian, firmly, 'No, we're going on with the auction! Not because it would cost money to postpone, Barney. And not because I'm a stubborn old SOB who doesn't give a damn about his family. We're holding that sale because it's our way of telling the world that Parajians is going on.'

'But –'

'But what, Harriet?' he interrupted. 'Veron and Hector are dead. We can't bring them back to life. We've got to look to the future. And that's Parajians! Not just for you and me. But for Mark and Gregory and Sara! Yes, and Stephen too!'

Despite herself, Harriet responded to this appeal. Nonetheless, she said: 'That's fine, Paul. But you're skimming over a lot, aren't you? There have been two murders. How do we know what to expect?'

Paul became patriarchal. 'We don't know what happened and we don't know what's going to happen. Mark told me he would face his problems one at a time – today's problems today, and tomorrow's tomorrow. He's right. Behaving any other way is foolish – or cowardly!'

While Harriet sat silent, Barney caught fire. His head told him that Paul was stubborn as an ox. But his foot was tapping out the martial tempo of 'Stouthearted Men.'

Sara's encounter with pessimism was altogether less predictable.

'I'm meeting Mr Parajian,' she informed the head-waiter, ignoring the avid glint the name produced.

French was *de rigueur* at La Cheminée, but they could read newspapers all right. Threading her way through the obligatory lunchtime gloom, Sara felt every eye was on her.

'Hi, Gregory,' she said, reaching the table at last. 'Yes, a martini, straight up ...'

Then, ignoring the circles under Gregory's eyes and the menu lying unopened beside his drink, she took a deep breath. 'Thank God, the Sloan has finally settled the whole mess about Veron! When I called Mark last night, he said it would still take time before we get the money – and the stock. That's a shame ...' Anxiety about Green Thumbs nearly swung her off course, but she caught herself in time. 'Maybe our luck is finally changing.'

Gregory was listening but not hearing. He waited until she finished, then addressed the waiter. 'Yes, I think we're ready to order now.'

Behind the cardboard barricade, Sara chose Steak Tartare at random. Why, she wondered, had Gregory invited her to lunch if not to discuss the letter from Everett Gabler?

'I wanted to talk to you,' he said when the waiter departed, 'about Corinne's wedding. With everything that's happened, I think Mark and Helen should ask her to postpone it.'

Sara almost choked over her drink. Whatever she had expected, it was not this. 'You mean the publicity?'

'What else could I mean?' he retorted irritably.

Sara knew she had been spared the full brunt of the

sensationalism. Last night Mark had described the curiosity-seekers trooping in and out of the store. Consciously making allowances, she said: 'Well, it's Corinne's decision, isn't it? Helen says she doesn't seem to care – '

'Lois thinks she should care!' he shot back. 'Corinne's a member of the Parajian family, isn't she?'

Although she was not hungry, Sara was glad to see lunch arrive. Now she could resist some acid comments about family feeling, with special reference to Lois. Mark's sons were the ones who played with young Stephen. Lois' daughters saw him once a year.

'Maybe you should talk to Daddy about it,' she suggested sardonically.

'I already have. We were talking about weddings – '

'What did he say?' Sara could not imagine the scene.

'He told me,' said her brother with a tight grin, 'to mind my own business.'

Odd notions began assailing Sara, including the possibility that Gregory was having a nervous breakdown. 'What do you mean? You just happened to be talking about weddings?'

'Maybe it was those pictures of Hector's,' Gregory replied reflectively. 'I got thinking about one thing and another. Do you remember that story of Grandmother's about how she went with Paul to buy the ring?'

'No, I don't,' said Sara, more sharply than she intended. By common consent, she and her brothers rarely mentioned that other life. Greece and Grandmother conjured up too many bitter memories.

'Paul remembered,' said Gregory, almost sadly. 'Naturally, he would.'

With this, he fell into a reverie that chilled Sara to the bone. Only occasionally did the horrors of the past reach out to shadow her busy, contented life. First Paul and Harriet, then Alex, had blocked off the refugee camp, the strangers, the hunger.

What had brought it all back for Gregory?

She felt her way. 'How are things at the store?' she asked cautiously. 'I talked to Mark last night, but I haven't seen Daddy for days. Harriet says he's all wrapped up with the auction.'

Nervousness almost made her gabble, but Gregory was far away.

'Dad?' he said, shaking himself back into the present. 'Oh, he's the same as ever. To hell with publicity! To hell with murders! Parajians is going to have the sale of the century! That's his way of doing things. You ought to know that!'

'I do!' Sara cried, as hotly as if this were a criticism. 'And I admire him for it.'

'We all admire him,' said Gregory evenly. 'But that doesn't mean he isn't getting older. He's not the man he was twenty or thirty years ago.'

Sara felt a burden lift. 'You mean we should start thinking about what we're going to do once we get Veron's stock?' she said, hoping for firm footing.

'Veron's stock?' Gregory echoed vaguely. 'Oh God, Sara! We've got a hell of a lot to get through before we reach Veron's stock!'

'You're telling me!' she flashed back. 'Alex and I have got a payroll to meet!'

Too late, she bit her lip. Gregory was even worse than Mark when it came to Alex and Green Thumbs.

'Dad will bail you out,' said Gregory in a voice she disliked. 'He always has, hasn't he?'

'And I suppose you're going to try to talk him out of it!' she cried in a flare of alarm.

'Me?' said Gregory somberly. 'Hell, no! We've got to stick together now. Otherwise too many people could get hurt. Things aren't the way they used to be. There's no use pretending. You can only live a lie so long.'

'I don't know what you're talking about,' she said flatly.

'You avoid a lot of trouble that way, Sara, don't you?' Then, with new decision, he went on: 'And, by God, you might be right! Maybe that's the position we should all take.'

Before she could reply, he picked up his fork and resolutely began a long anecdote about the Parke-Bernet Gallery.

17. Some Loquacious Vessels

An eminent jurist once observed that a word is only the skin of a living thought. Its color and content vary with time and circumstance.

So does its clout.

The public went from headlines (PARAJIAN AIDE MURDERED) to inner-page driblets (INVESTIGATION CONTINUING SAY POLICE), to feature-fiction (IS THERE AN ARMENIAN MAFIA?). Meanwhile, more traditional reading matter was available. Like all classics, it was not only read but reread.

Mr and Mrs Mark Parajian
request the pleasure of your company
at the marriage of their daughter
Corinne Virginia . . .

In Hempstead, close study of the text had uncovered problem after problem. Had all Parajian salesmen been invited to Amagansett, or just a chosen few? If Arthur Sourian had been singled out, did that imply a promotion? Was a Waring blender too much or too little? And, most important of all, would a pink pantsuit do for an August wedding?

Such innocent complications were enough to send Mavis Sourian to the telephone and a good, solid hour with her sister in Forest Hills.

On Central Park South, Lois Parajian had long since instructed Cartier's to monogram a demitasse set. But she was seeking sisterly counsel too.

'You know how they are, Lee,' she told San Francisco. 'The wedding is bad enough, but there's no use even talking to them about it. If you ask me, they want to get her married off before anything else happens . . . What? Oh, I'm sure Helen understands you've been planning this trip to Tahiti for ages ... Hmm? ... No, you can never have too many towels – if they use towels in a camper ... Yes ... yes, I think so too, but as I was saying, at least the wedding won't have every Tom, Dick and Harry. But this auction makes me want to scream ... In the *Chronicle*? No, I haven't seen the paper yet.' Lois sighed affectedly at Lee's next question. Then, with iron gaiety: 'Gregory? Fine, just fine. Oh, he isn't enjoying this uproar any more than I am, but otherwise he's fine.'

Most sisters have perfected the art of exchanging confidences without overt disloyalty to their mates. Lee was now able to tell her husband that something was wrong with Gregory. Dinner would be over in San Francisco before she discovered that he did not care.

And Lois was in a position to cite Lee as a sample of West Coast opinion. Without downing the receiver, she began dialing.

Barney Olender answered the phone.

'Gregory? No, he's not around, Lois,' he said chattily. 'How did you like our announcement in the *Times*? Pretty classy, huh?'

Excellent taste, Lee had said. For *them*.

'Lovely,' said Lois distantly. 'Will you ask Gregory to call me when he gets in?'

'I'll leave a note on his desk,' Barney promised. 'But he hasn't been in all day, so I don't know when to expect him. Say, Gregory's all right, isn't he, Lois? I thought he looked kind of under the weather yesterday.'

'He's catching a cold,' Lois lied. 'Thank you, Barney.'

But she was frowning when she finally reached for the *Times*.

'Parajians,' the advertisement ran with Miss Mintz's austerity, 'announces an auction of Oriental rugs. At the Sotheby Parke-Bernet Galleries ...'

In Lansing, Admiral Christiansen barely glanced at it. He was still deep in the catalog, covering margins with indecipherable hen tracks. In other cities, however, men and women studied the words and were transported by dreams of glory straight into Xanadu.

Ken Nicolls, on the other hand, was cannonballed into Charlie Trinkam.

Ken's *Times* had been folded into that compact rectangle mastered only by subway regulars, so that a turn of the wrist had revealed Parajians' solitary, quarter-page splendor. Since yearning and a disciplined exit from the IRT are incompatible, this led to a collision.

'Whuf! Sorry – oh, it's you, Nicolls. You'd better move faster than that around here,' Charlie advised, sweeping him along. 'Otherwise you'll get trampled to death. What's in the paper, anyway? Are they trying truth drugs over at Combustion Engineering?'

Even on his own time, Ken was defensive about Oriental rugs.

'Just happened to catch the story,' he muttered, trying to remember what the *Times* had said about corporate leaks.

Charlie had eyes like a hawk. 'Oh, the Parajians ad. Boy, that auction had better be a lulu. Otherwise Commercial Credit is going to pull the plug.'

On the sixth floor, Everett Gabler had dismissed Xanadu in favor of his kind of document. He was reading Veron Aratounian's death certificate, finally issued by the New York City Department of Health. At long last, probate of an estate likely to run into seven figures could commence.

'Paul Parajian wants a copy for those lawyers in Teheran who are holding her will,' he informed Thatcher while they awaited a distinguished visitor. 'I am tempted to take it over there myself.'

Although temptation is a chronic occupational hazard for bankers, Thatcher was not unduly worried. 'The Sloan has a roomful of messengers for that purpose, Everett,' he pointed out, checking his watch.

The Minister of Economic Development, Republic of India, was twenty minutes late. Since Bradford Withers, president of the Sloan Guaranty Trust, was his escort, this was only to be expected. Withers might be a notable world traveler, but there were still vast tracts of the Sloan that were virgin territory to him.

Any minute now, Installment Credit would be on the line, asking Thatcher to collect his strays.

'With the death certificate,' said Everett, 'I could well include some advice which I can scarcely put in writing.'

'That must be some advice.' Thatcher kept his comment casual, although he could see how serious Everett was. Tardiness and Bradford Withers were usually good for a Gablerian blast.

'It is only right that the Parajians should be warned not to expect immediate disbursement.'

'You mean that the courts are notoriously reluctant to let a murderer profit from his victim's estate? Well, the Sloan is too.'

In this instance, Everett did not like calling a spade a spade.

'We must certainly resign ourselves to further delay in probate,' he replied, avoiding specifics, 'in addition to the ... er, delays we have already encountered.'

Thatcher considered this and thought he saw some light. 'Has Mrs Daniels been asking you for an advance again? Or Mrs Gregory Parajian? She's a lady who believes in moral pressure, I recall. Now that they've received your letter, I imagine they're both quite impatient.'

Gabler gave the devil his due. Since the authentication of Mrs Aratounian, communications between the Sloan and the Parajians had been minimal.

'Except this call from Paul Parajian, whose behavior has been impeccable throughout.'

Miss Corsa, who had entered in time to hear this rare tribute, looked respectful, as well she might. But she had news from her scouts. Mr Withers and the Minister of Economic Development had just been sighted nearing Coin and Currency.

'If only it were deference to India's interest in gold,' said Thatcher. 'But I'm afraid that's where Brad thinks my office is. You'd better send somebody after them. By the way, why aren't we meeting up in the tower?'

Mr Withers' suite, Miss Corsa reminded him before leaving to find a bloodhound, was redecorated every August.

Everett could not let that pass. 'This must be the first summer in years that Withers has seen even the outside of the Sloan,' he observed with perfect justice.

But with ten minutes in hand, Thatcher proposed to clear some decks.

'If the Parajians aren't on your back, Everett,' he said severely, 'precisely why do you contemplate injecting yourself?'

Uncharacteristically, Everett temporized. 'We at the Sloan have a duty.'

'Ye-es?'

'A duty which makes me entertain the possibility that the Sloan will vote the shares of Parajian stock we hold in trust.' Everett began warming up. 'Already several questions have been left in limbo – questions about managerial policy and decision-making. I am concerned about them, and I am anxious that further delays do not materially violate Mrs Aratounian's clearly stated testamentary intentions. We may have an obligation to intervene, in order to be sure that any actions taken now have a beneficial effect on the estate.'

No bank hurls itself lightly into a mincing machine. Thatcher knew this. And so, despite the loftiness, did Everett. But for years he had labored in Mrs Aratounian's behalf. He had done everything humanly possible to ensure her an old age free from want. And what had happened? In her hour of need, she had been struck down at his feet. Even her identity had been impugned. Everett Gabler had ceased to be a trust officer and become her champion.

Thatcher picked his way with care. 'I appreciate your opinion, Everett. And the occasion for such activity may arise. But until it does, I think we had better follow out standard procedure.'

How could he know that a whole subcontinent was waiting to trip him up?

'Ah, John,' said Bradford Withers, making him sound like Dr Livingstone. 'And Gabler. Your Excellency, may I present ...'

The Minister of Economic Development proved to be a small, tidy man looking utterly baffled. The reason was soon apparent. Dr Roy had been a distinguished statistician before political elevation. Nothing in his profession, let alone his religion, had prepared him for Bradford Withers.

'... very interesting old dollar bills,' Brad was confiding.

'As well as Continentals. And there's a nice display of Confederate money, too. I didn't even know we had them. They got me thinking, John. It might be a nice gesture to assemble a set and present it to Mrs Gandhi.'

'Yes indeed,' said Thatcher neutrally. He wished Dr Roy did not look so compassionate.

'Well, we'll have to get together to discuss it. Now I'll leave you to hammer out the details of your contract.' said Brad, a summit man if ever there was one.

In point of fact, a whole trade mission from India was going to meet a phalanx of Sloan technicians in the near future. Only a Withers could believe that you financed an integrated rolling mill over drinks with a Tata.

Nevertheless, a climate of agreement is always useful, and Everett, who would be heading up the Sloan team, made good use of his hour with the Minister. Cost overruns, payment schedules and Eurodollars lasted until exactly the moment scheduled for Brad's return.

This time the wait had to be filled with stately small talk.

Yes, the Minister was finding his trip profitable.

Yes, Mr Gabler was looking forward to his visit to India.

Yes, it certainly was hot.

Thatcher was about to dispatch another posse when the Minister riveted him.

'... using the joint-venture form, of course. We anticipate government-sponsored looms, while Parajians would provide the distribution system. There is a great potential in expanding Indian rug production.'

'Ah, all set are we?'

It would be a grave error to tell Bradford Withers that they had barely begun. The less he knew about trade missions the better.

Outside of India, however, the damage had been done.

'An interesting and well-informed man, for a public official,' Everett began deceptively. 'I foresee some difficulty in connection with these subcontract provisions.'

Thatcher, who could foresee more immediate difficulties, waited.

'And you no doubt heard that reference to Indian rugs? Under the circumstances, John, I feel it incumbent on us to inquire more closely into what is currently happening at Parajians. We may not decide it is necessary to vote our stock – but we may find a situation where it is absolutely essential. At the very least, we must take a long, hard look at the management situation.'

Thatcher was already checking the calendar that Miss Corsa kept so rigorously. But Everett did not relax until he put his acquiescence into so many words:

'You win, Everett. I'll be free to join you tomorrow afternoon.'

18. To the Treasure House

'What is *he* doing here?'

Thatcher had not expected melodrama within seconds of entering Parajians the following day, but here was Everett, pointing like a bird dog.

The culprit was Ken Nicolls, deep in conclave with a salesman.

'You recall that Nicolls is considering a rug, don't you, Everett? Besides, this is his lunch hour,' said Thatcher, hoping this last was accurate.

Everett remembered Nicolls and his Oriental, all right. With policemen invading the Sloan, he was never going to forget. He arrived in time to hear Arthur Sourian saying:

'... a very nice, versatile Sena. I think you'd be very happy with it. And Mrs Nicolls will enjoy it too.'

'How much?' Ken demanded forthrightly.

'This Sena is – let me see – twenty-six hundred dollars.'

'Too much,' said Ken without hesitation. For once he had done the right thing.

'Ah, Nicolls,' purred Gabler. 'Bargaining hard, are you?'

Ken swung around in horror. Unexpected encounters with superiors are almost as bad as unexpected encounters with the police.

Furthermore, Everett was a past master of horse trading.

Arthur Sourian was nobody's fool. 'Not only is this Sena an excellent investment,' he said, deftly incorporating Gabler and Thatcher into his audience, 'it is very economical floor covering. It will last ten times as long as any wall-to-wall carpeting.'

Sourian could scarcely be expected to know he was preaching to a hooked-rug aficionado.

Fortunately, before they could clash over the nature of investments, there was a welcome interruption.

'Arthur!' Sara Daniels paused, then in an outpouring of exuberance ran forward to embrace him. 'How are you? How's Mavis?'

She was hugging him when she caught sight of the others.

'Why, Mr Gabler! And Mr Thatcher! I didn't see you. Alex, look who's here!'

Alex Daniels was beaming as he pumped hands. Mr and Mrs Daniels were walking on air, and didn't care who knew it.

Thatcher had seen many people leave the Sloan this way, usually with a fat check from Commercial Credit in their pocket. He proceeded to test his theory.

'I hope you were pleased to get our letter, Mrs Daniels. You see, the first step did not take as long as you feared.'

He need not have been so circumspect.

'Oh, there's no hurry. Take all the time you want,' she said cheerfully.

Alex adopted a more long-range view. 'Of course, we want to get things settled sometime. But the crisis is over. Paul has just come to the rescue.'

'Green Thumbs is going to stay in business for quite a while,' Sara said happily. 'It may not be as big as Parajians, but at least it's our own.'

She gazed around unresentfully. Parajians might emphasize quiet dignity, but in plain view, three salesmen were writing up sales, two customers were promising to bring back their wives and more than one *Sold* tag attested to a brisk morning's trade.

'I see Khassim's murder hasn't scared anyone away,' Alex remarked.

'Far from it,' Arthur Sourian replied. 'The first few days, everybody in New York was in and out of here. But we're back to normal now. Or even a little better than normal.'

'You can have it,' said Alex sarcastically. 'We'll stick to the production end. It may have its drawbacks, but we're safe from the great American public.'

Possibly he had forgotten he was talking to bankers, a salesman and a customer. Possibly he was too jubilant to care.

'Alex,' said Sara, 'we promised Nelson we'd meet him at two o'clock.'

Mention of time acted like a solvent.

'And I've got to get back to work,' said Ken Nicolls, bolting.

Everett headed for the elevator. 'So Walter Bowman was right,' he said. 'Paul Parajian really is underwriting this Green Thumbs, or whatever they may call it.'

'Walter's not usually wrong,' said Thatcher mildly. 'Did you think he was this time?'

'These greenhouses,' said Everett, paraphrasing Bowman freely, 'are not a genuine business. They're merely an expensive hobby.'

Thatcher felt forced to take issue. 'Well, there's nothing sinister in that, Everett. Fathers have been shelling out to their daughters' husbands ever since the dawn of history.'

Thatcher's son-in-law was an extremely successful surgeon. But once he had been a tyro, opening his first office. Ben and Laura remembered the anxiety of those youthful beginnings. Thatcher remembered the exact amount of the tab.

'Whatever anybody else may suggest,' he continued, 'this family certainly acts like a family.'

He received corroboration as soon as they stepped into Paul Parajian's office.

Mark rose immediately and said: 'Before we get started, Mr Gabler, my wife made me promise to ask if you're coming. She says we don't have your reply.'

'Good heavens! I know we sent it!' Chagrin led Everett to courtliness. 'Please make my apologies to Mrs Parajian. I am indeed coming. My secretary already knows that nothing is to interfere.'

'And she said to tell you Corinne is thrilled with your decanter.'

Paul Parajian was indulgent. 'You see what's really important around here,' he told Thatcher. 'Mark's girl is getting married and she's the first grandchild to go.'

Even without prior knowledge, Thatcher would have guessed. Every trust officer is an honorary uncle when it comes to weddings. The Sloan had instituted a budget for gifts.

In the subsequent fifteen minutes, Everett skillfully modulated from the theme of nuptials to the theme of death. Smoothly he coasted into the Health Department certificate.

'Here it is,' he said. 'However, the Sloan must add a caution ...'

Thatcher could not see any significant reaction. Both Paul Parajian and Mark were unmoved by Everett's diplomatic reminder that they were all still embroiled in a murder investigation.

Everett's first suggestion that the Sloan might become their acting partner woke them up.

'Gregory should hear this too,' Paul interrupted. 'Mark, didn't you tell him to come?'

'I had them leave a message on his desk.'

'Well, try again!' Parajian said abruptly. 'I want him to hear this from the bank – not through one of us.'

'There's nothing to worry about – '

Parajian did not let him finish. 'Forget about worrying, and just get him in here!'

Scowling, Mark went to obey. But an extended stint on the phone was fruitless. He was still glowering when he returned to his seat and broke in on Everett's catechism about India.

'No luck,' he said tersely. 'They don't know where he is.'

'What do you mean? Did you talk to his secretary?'

'Yes.'

'What did she – '

'She doesn't know,' Mark broke in.

Paul Parajian was deaf to warnings, no matter how clear. 'Maybe he's sick. Call Lois.'

'We tried to call Lois,' he explained. 'Nobody's home. Let's just go on and we'll fill Greg in later.'

Parajian stared for a moment, then belatedly responded to his cue. 'That's a shame. Gregory's probably over at Parke-Bernet.'

Thatcher doubted it, but both he and Gabler were too experienced to probe.

'As I was saying,' Gabler addressed Mark, 'the voting situation has not altered. There is still danger of a stalemate at a critical juncture. In that case, the Sloan might be compelled to break the deadlock.'

'You can forget about stalemates,' Paul Parajian said authoritatively.

'That's right,' agreed Mark.

Everett sat still – a technique that was often more effective than a third degree. It was Mark Parajian, not his father, who succumbed.

'We've reached a compromise,' he volunteered. When his father nodded, he added sourly: 'It's the usual kind around here. Paul has budged one inch while Sara and I have given up ten miles.'

Paul Parajian looked complacent until Gabler asked, 'And Mr Gregory Parajian?'

'Gregory's share by itself is too small to make any difference,' Paul said. 'Besides, he's always half liked the sound of India and Pakistan.'

Thatcher wondered if Mark always played the tortoise to Gregory's hare.

Meanwhile, Everett was continuing his cross-examination. 'I would be interested to hear the details of your plans.'

With undisguised gusto, Paul plunged into a description of the gold mine waiting in India and Pakistan. Then, with a mocking glance at his son, he said: 'But that's part of our compromise. Expansion depends on the auction and how well we do with it.'

'And there's no telling about that,' Mark said stolidly. 'With economic disruption all over the world, people aren't going to be so free and easy with their bidding.'

Paul had already won this argument. 'My kind of people will,' he said confidently. 'But you see, Gabler, this auction will be the big test. Everyone's waiting to see if the old man has lost his touch.'

He bared his teeth in a broad smile. Whatever else he might be concerned with, Paul Parajian had no doubts about his own judgement.

'We're not deciding anything until we see how the auction

goes,' Mark insisted. 'And there are still plenty of ifs about that. I'll say one thing. People may not do a lot of high bidding, but they'll see a collection that will knock their eyes out.'

Paul Parajian was climbing to his feet. 'Mark's the one who did the buying,' he said, generously. 'Now I've got to do my part. If I don't get up to Parke-Bernet, there won't be any auction.'

Mark settled down to work as everybody else prepared to leave. His last suggestion came as he was frowning over a staggering bill from Cosmo Medici Graphic Consultants.

'Do you want to take my car, Paul? It's in the garage.'

'The wagon or the sports car?' Parajian asked from the doorway.

Mark shrugged. 'It's the Porsche. Why don't you take it? It'll get you uptown in half the time.'

'Not on your life. I'm too old to learn to use things like tachometers and floor shifts.'

For a moment Mark shed his cares. 'Just because Paul pushed a hack when he was young and poor,' he grinned, 'he thinks he's got a duty to enrich the cabbies of New York.'

'I'm off to enrich one myself,' said Thatcher, departing in the wake of Gabler and Parajian.

'Mark's always been conservative,' said Parajian in the elevator. 'But you can reason with him, if you've got time. He just doesn't like anything new and different. But he gets used to things. Before you know it, he'll stop being so edgy and turn into a big booster.'

There was no sign of this transformation when Gregory Parajian strolled through the door an hour later.

'Where the hell have you been?' Mark exploded. 'We've been looking all over for you.'

Gregory shrugged. 'Just taking care of a few personal matters.'

'You sure picked a great time to go spinning off! This auction is going to be bad enough, but if you don't do your part we're really going to take a beating.'

'All right, all right,' said Gregory with a gesture of surrender. 'Keep your shirt on, Mark. Your little brother is here and ready to roll up his sleeves. I guarantee you'll have every important buyer in the country at Parke-Bernet.'

'I hope so,' Mark grunted.

'Come on, Mark, that's not what's eating you. We'll get a big crowd. The question is whether they'll be willing to spend.'

Mollified, Mark grimaced across the desk. 'Where were you when I needed you? You should have heard Paul telling it to the Sloan. As far as he's concerned, the auction is over and we're already buying up half of India. It was one of his better performances.'

Gregory was sympathetic. 'I know what you mean. When Paul goes into his act, he gives it everything he's got. So far he hasn't made any mistakes.' He paused, then said wryly, 'And as long as he's in the saddle, let's hope he can keep it up.'

19. Ah, Take the Cash

Time is notoriously wayward, but even red-letter days do ultimately arrive.

The moment he emerged from the taxi in front of the Sotheby Parke-Bernet Galleries, John Thatcher sensed he was attending a very special event. The usual tide of life on upper Madison Avenue was rolling along the sidewalk: suburban matrons bent on boutiques, gourmets in search of the perfect shallot. But cutting across the tide, like a school of sharks, were the men headed for the Parajian auction. They came from taxis and buses, from the subway and from limousines. Inside they evinced the same single-mindedness – brushing past the chaste announcement of today's sale, ignoring the schedule of forthcoming sales, in order to converge on the elevator.

Of course, there could be two interpretations for the crowd.

'You might say they're here to witness the fall of a titan,' said Thatcher. 'But I doubt it. This already has the smell of success.'

His two companions agreed. Everett Gabler had to rely on general financial intuition, but Walter Bowman drew on experience. That morning he had confessed to being a regular at New York's major galleries.

'You can learn a lot at these special sales,' he had explained. 'I like to keep an eye on where the money is.'

Now he paused at the portieres of the main room and cast a knowledgeable glance over the occupants.

'Not as many Japanese this year,' he announced. 'I guess they're really hurting where it counts.'

But Japanese or no, the international community was more than adequately represented. English might be the lingua franca of the day, but it was English in many guises. Thatcher heard the guttural accents of Munich, the breathy elisions of Paris and the piping precision of Oxford. The jets had been landing prospective purchasers at Kennedy Airport for days. And here they sat, catalogs in hand, chatting to each other with the camaraderie of a closed profession.

Everett Gabler had been making some calculations. 'Do you realize how much money it took to assemble this group in one city?'

'Yes indeed,' said Thatcher. 'Pan Am is going to make money, even if the Parajians don't.'

Just then, Bowman returned from an exploratory circuit of the room to protect his seat against a late arrival. He was excited.

'Boy, they've got everybody. Do you see that one in uniform?'

Thatcher and Gabler craned their necks to catch a glimpse of a spry, white-haired gentleman in brown cotton fatigues.

'That's the People's Republic,' Bowman told them. 'Apparently Parajian has got one old Chinese rug they want.'

That was the new Orient, thought Thatcher – a declining Japanese attendance and the first tendrils of a mightier presence. He reminded himself to have a talk with International Division as soon as he returned to the Sloan.

The sale began casually. Unheralded, a small rug appeared, the auctioneer assumed his stance and, with no abatement in the overall conversational level, a sale at fifteen hundred dollars was effected. In the row ahead, the two emissaries from Munich did not bother to look up.

'Good heavens, isn't anybody interested?' Gabler asked. 'What did they come for?'

Even as he spoke the transaction was being duplicated.

'They're just tuning up the orchestra,' Bowman reassured him. 'You'll be able to tell when they get to the serious stuff.'

He was quite right. After forty-five minutes, an assistant appeared with a rug that, to the uninitiated, looked exactly the same as its predecessors. As if by magic, backs straightened, catalogs flicked open and a hush descended.

'A very nice little prayer rug,' the auctioneer said nonchalantly. 'An antique Tabriz measuring four by six.'

'Three thousand,' snapped an aggressive voice before the auctioneer's mouth had fully closed.

'Do I hear four thousand?'

He heard not only four, but five and six in rapid succession. The Tabriz was finally knocked down at six thousand eight hundred, after a snarling progression through the final five hundred dollars. Walter Bowman sighed with appreciation.

'Well, there's your overture,' he muttered.

'I can scarcely wait for the main aria,' Thatcher retorted.

But the Parajians and the gallery had orchestrated this occasion as carefully as any composer. The auctioneer industriously disposed of the prayer rugs – first the singles, then those that were doubly and trebly arched. Every now and then he let fall a tantalizing hint of delights to come. An antique Marasali had many excellences.

'... but not the equal of the more important Marasali that will appear after the break,' he said blandly. 'Nonetheless, a classic example of ...'

A Sarouk that provoked a demented display of competition was dismissed as a superior specimen of color-aging in wool. 'The silks,' the auctioneer added, 'will be presented later.'

Thatcher respectfully watched the prices rise. The buyer from Munich hurled himself into the fray at the sight of a six-by-ten Koula. Ten minutes later – and ten thousand dollars poorer – he had to unburden himself to somebody.

'It is better that I buy when I can,' he rasped, ferociously amiable. 'In another hour, I will not be able to afford anything.'

Like every banker, Thatcher knew all about auction fever. But it was a malady endemic to amateurs. He had yet to see commercial dealers gripped by the hysteria. Cautiously, he asked his newfound friend why the bidding was so high.

'It is high when measured by the past. But everybody here must plan in terms of the future. It is possible that this may be the last time a collection of this quality is offered on the open market. There are those who think so.'

'And do you?' asked Thatcher.

There was an immense shrug. 'I don't know. But I do know that Paul Parajian thinks so, and that is enough for my museum.'

Everett Gabler had been following every word. Under cover of the next round of bidding, he said, 'That is a remarkable tribute to Parajian.'

Bowman phrased it differently. 'Boy, that's the way to make a market,' he said admiringly. 'Get everybody to believe you're the Great White Father who knows all.'

'S-sh!' hissed his neighbors.

'I have here a rather unusual item for this collection,' the auctioneer announced as two assistants struggled forward under their load. 'It will be the only Chinese rug shown today, and ...'

Within moments it was evident that a duel was under way. After a few *pro forma* incursions into the arena, all Occidentals retired to their role as spectators.

'I have eleven thousand from Mr Takamara. Mr Li, do I hear ... ?

'Mr Li has offered eleven five. Now I have twelve ...'

And finally:

'Going once, going twice, sold to Mr Li for thirteen five. We will now adjourn for half an hour.'

Thatcher enjoyed a good first-act curtain as well as the next man. 'That's a very nice note on which to break,' he remarked. 'As I understand it, we have yet to see any of the real treasures.'

'That's right,' said someone who was surging down the aisle after him. Mark Parajian was so elated he was stammering. 'My God, it can't hold up this way. Do you realize we're getting prices that have never been seen before?'

'I think everybody here understands that,' Gabler replied.

Mark's face lit up. 'If my arithmetic is right, we've already cleared a profit.'

Gabler was not prepared to indulge the delusion that his own arithmetic could be faulty. 'You have,' he said firmly.

'We'd better get some coffee.' Mark was steering them to an anteroom already crowded to capacity. 'But as far as I'm concerned, we could break out the champagne now. Isn't that right, Greg?'

All the Parajians were smiling so hard today it must have

hurt. Gregory and Sara greeted the Sloan contingent as if they were long-lost friends.

'It's unbelievable,' said Sara, dispensing coffee with a blind eye.

'And wait until later,' Greg promised jubilantly.

Mark was determined not to be precipitate. 'You can't expect it to go on. Why, if it did ...' He broke off, speechless at the prospect.

'It will. The time to be a prophet of doom has passed.' Gregory slapped his brother on the shoulder. 'Paul was right all the way. In fact, he always has been.'

'Look, is it likely that I'm going to knock him now? All I'm saying is that – '

'Good morning, Admiral,' said Sara, loud and clear. 'Isn't the sale going splendidly?'

Recalled to their social duties, Mark and Gregory turned. Admiral Christiansen, resplendent in a white linen suit, advanced with flags flying.

'Where's Paul?' he demanded.

Harriet had overheard the question. 'He's over there, talking with Dr Barnes about the Bakshaish that's coming up later. You may have trouble getting through to him.'

Following her pointed finger, Christiansen nodded sagely. 'Building up interest, eh?' he said. 'Paul's got a good head on his shoulders. Well, I'll congratulate him later. I haven't seen a sale like this since Paris in 1939 ...'

His audience, variously gratified and respectful, was suddenly enlarged. Barney Olender came into sight, stern first.

'Excuse me ... Admiral! Admiral Christiansen. Well, talk about the devil!' he burbled, clasping Christiansen's hand.

The Admiral did not seem to mind the allusion. 'Why, Barney Olender,' he said with creaky geniality. 'This is a great day for you too, isn't it?'

'You've got to admit we've come a long way.' Barney was so overjoyed that he playfully punched Christiansen's forearm.

The specter of *lèse-majesté* loomed, but Christiansen took no offense. 'I'd never have believed it,' he chortled back at Barney.

'Between you and me,' said Barney, ignoring the circle of listeners, 'neither would I!'

The two of them grinned foolishly at each other.

'Boy, was I scared when I went to Lansing that time,' Barney reminisced at large. 'It was Paul's first shipment, and I didn't know a thing about rugs. Imagine trying to sell Admiral Christiansen! Talk about being outclassed!'

'Ho, ho!' said Christiansen, while everybody else smiled sycophantically. 'I wouldn't have given a plugged nickel for Parajians' chances in those days. I want to tell Paul myself.'

'Let's see if we can't get through to him now,' said Gregory, escorting him away. 'I know he'll want to see you, Admiral.'

Mark and Sara moved on to other duties, while Harriet remained only long enough to say: 'I'm so happy for Paul. I don't know how this auction ever became such a test, but it's been weighing on me for weeks.'

An hour later, Thatcher was deciding that nobody would ever dare test Paul Parajian again. The Bakshaish, which turned out to be a nineteenth-century bird carpet, had just been acquired by Dr Barnes – after spirited attacks from every corner of the room – for the nice round sum of forty-five thousand dollars.

'Texas money,' came a disgruntled whisper from the row ahead. 'What chance does the little man have?'

The little man in question was not getting much of Thatcher's sympathy. He had just topped a bid of fifty thousand dollars for a rug hailed as the equal of the famous Ardebil in the Victoria and Albert Museum.

'What can they be saving for the grand finale?' whispered Bowman.

'I'm almost afraid to guess. For all I know, Parajian has robbed the Grand Mosque.'

Perhaps he had. The auctioneer brazenly predicted that many in the room would consider Parajians' last offering as the greatest rug ever seen in the Western world.

'A sixteenth-century imperial Ushak mosque carpet measuring twenty-eight feet by fifteen feet,' he intoned reverently. 'Combining a rare ruby with sapphire blue, the center well covered with small medallions, the borders unique in their complexity. Please note the maker's name woven into the lower corner ...'

For some, Paul Parajian's finest hour may have come when the stunned assemblage looked, absorbed, then burst into spontaneous applause. For some, it may have been when the rug finally sold to an anonymous dealer-agent for a sum in excess of one hundred thousand dollars. For Everett Gabler, it was certainly when he completed his internal addition and concluded that the Sloan Guaranty Trust would be well advised to support Paul Parajian in his Far East venture.

But John Thatcher preferred to pinpoint a different vignette. It came later, amidst the popping of champagne corks and the torrent of congratulations. Paul Parajian, his left arm draped around his wife, his right hand lofting his glass on high, offered a toast:

'To Parajians!' he boomed. 'May it live forever!'

20. And Let the Credit Go

Winning may not be everything, but it beats losing.

'Listen to this, Harriet!' Paul urged at breakfast the next morning without looking up from his *Times*. '"The record price paid for Parajians' rare Ushak has triggered speculation about the buyer. Rumors in rug circles include Sheik Yadami of Abu Dhabi, the Metropolitan Museum and Olympia Venner" ... Who the hell is Olympia Venner?'

'That actress,' Harriet replied, buttering toast.

Paul had already continued: '"Prices significantly higher than those at this spring's Sotheby sale in London, are attributed to increased interest in Orientals, as well as the unusual quality of the Parajian collection. Admiral Homer Christiansen, noted author and expert ..."'

Harriet did not normally like being read aloud to, but today was an exception.

'Wonderful!' she exclaimed when Paul concluded.

'It's the cream in our coffee,' he declared.

'Now you sound like Barney,' she said, smiling. She hummed a few bars of that great old song.

He recognized the spirit, if not the tune. 'I can hardly wait to get to the store today.'

'Get to the store – !' She put down her cup. 'You're not going to work today? Surely, now that the auction is over, you can take some time off. I thought maybe we could have a long weekend in Amagansett. Besides, you need some rest and relaxation before the wedding sweeps over us ...'

Her speech trailed off. Suggesting rest and relaxation to Paul was always a waste of breath. Hammocks in the shade always took a poor second to working.

'I suppose you're going to start right away with all that complicated dickering about India,' she said with mocking exasperation.

'No, that's tomorrow,' he admitted. 'The boys and I will start working up a proposal. But today' – he shook his head with vast contentment – 'today's no day to be away from Parajians!'

'Why?' she asked. Then, a residue of apprehension stirred. 'Gregory and Mark were just as thrilled as you were yesterday. And Sara, too!'

He honestly did not know what she was talking about. 'Of course they were,' he said. 'I never expected anything else. You think I want to crow over them? Hell, no. Listening to those bids yesterday was enough for me, and more! The reason I want to be at the store today – well, it's going to be a party for all of us!'

Wise woman that she was, Harriet recognized the truth when she heard it.

Arthur Sourian and Gregory were making a good start when Paul Parajian arrived.

'... the *Times*,' said Sourian, digging clippings out of a stuffed wallet. 'And the *Daily News* had a photograph, too. Not that it does the Ushak justice. But look!'

Obediently, Gregory did so. 'Newsprint isn't the best medium for Orientals,' he agreed.

Sourian was suffused with pride. 'No,' he said, carefully refolding, 'but all of them say that Parajians presented the finest collection of rugs ever auctioned in New York!'

If 'finest' meant 'most expensive,' he was right. Astronomical prices might capture the journalistic imagination, but excellence is an article of faith with merchandisers of nonessentials. Sourian devoutly believed that Parajian rugs were superior rugs. Otherwise he would have been working at Korvette's. To him and to everybody else on the floor, the auction was more than a commercial triumph. It was a substitute for that matchless imprimatur, tradition. From now on, the Parke-Bernet auction was going to be *Gold Medal at the Chicago Exposition*, *Founded in 1818*, and *Purveyor to HM the King*, all rolled up into one.

'Mavis was saying just this morning – Mr Parajian! Let me be the first to congratulate you!'

'I'll accept with thanks,' said Paul Parajian with a laugh. 'But you're not the first.'

Sure enough, a receiving line composed of half the firm's employees was just dispersing.

'Mark says it took him an hour to get upstairs to his office,' Gregory said. 'Everybody in the place wanted to tell him what a great buyer he is.'

'What they need is some customers,' said Paul forthrightly. 'That will get everybody back down to earth!'

'Oh, the customers will come, all right.'

Sourian went Gregory one better. 'There's Mrs Sparks!' he cried, sighting a prospect. 'My God, the news has reached Squaw Valley!'

'Mr Parajian,' said the assistant cashier worshipfully, 'I just had to tell you how pleased we all are!'

Gregory was beginning to yearn for the peace and quiet of his office. Once they had finally disentangled themselves, Paul inspected him.

'You've been working damned hard, Gregory. Why don't you take some time off? I know you're going to Europe this fall – but hell, why not take Lois up to Ontario for a couple of days? Do you both good!'

'Not right now,' Gregory replied temperately. 'I want to be on hand until we get all the deliveries out of the way.'

But mention of Lois had introduced an uncomfortable element of constraint.

After an internal struggle, Paul said impulsively, 'Look, Gregory, Lois realizes how important the auction was, doesn't she?'

Embarrassed, Gregory tried to make a joke. 'She's already basing big spending programs on it.'

'Fine,' said Paul emphatically. 'That means she won't be pressuring you anymore. All this business about kicking me out – no, let me finish – that was a reasonable difference of opinion. We should forget it! Parajians is on the brink of a new beginning – for all of us. I say, let bygones be bygones.'

Had he said too much? It appeared not.

'There's nothing I'd like better,' said Gregory fervently. 'Nothing!'

'Then that's exactly what we're going to do!'

The police had no such option.

'So, the rich get richer,' said Captain Muller dourly. He had no need of Arthur Sourian's clippings. Like the Sloan Guaranty Trust, Headquarters had sent observers to Parke-Bernet. 'I hope to Christ you didn't get swept off your feet and buy anything.'

Detective Loomis smiled dutifully and completed his report, which included the total grossed and the identity of the buyer of the Ushak.

'Which adds up to nothing,' Muller grunted.

'Unless it's important that the whole family was there, and they were all on the same side.' Arnie was still trying and still finding it heavy going. The murder investigations of Veron Aratounian and Hector Khassim were progressing in the technical sense only.

'Sure they were,' Muller snarled. 'They're not nuts. Whether they like it or not, that auction was important to them. They had to pretend everything was hunky-dory. I'll bet they'll be at each other's throats again within the week. But hell, I don't give a damn how much they tear each other apart – unless they do it with poison again!'

Detective Loomis was startled. 'You mean you think there might be another murder?'

'Look,' Muller retorted with savage patience. 'We don't know who killed the old lady and Khassim, do we? We don't know why they were killed. That's enough. I'm not looking into crystal balls.'

Arnie knew what was eating Muller. For all practical purposes, both cases were at a standstill.

'One thing we cleared up,' he ventured. 'That guy Alex Daniels – the husband – '

'I know who Daniels is,' said Muller irascibly.

'Remember how he and his wife said he left Parajians before

Khassim got murdered? Well, we've finally tracked down the guy he said he was meeting.'

Muller was tapping a pencil.

'Name of Herrick. He left that night on vacation. That's why we couldn't run him down until this morning. But he alibis Daniels. Says they met for lunch at the Yale Club. So that lets Daniels out of Khassim's murder, at least.'

There was a pregnant pause, and Arnie hurriedly added: 'Well, he looked good. He was broke, and he and his wife were the only ones who really needed Mrs Aratounian's money–'

'Great!' said Muller roundly. 'We've got a poison they all had access to. We've got a story about an impostor that peters out. Then we've got another story about a whole bunch of ringers – and we can't check it! We've got the makings of blackmail, and we don't have a clue what it's about. We've got pictures that don't make sense; we've got a half a dozen people who had all the opportunity in the world to commit one murder, or two. And what do you bring me?'

Arnie knew better than to tell him.

'Alex Daniels,' said Muller in disgust. 'The one man who couldn't have killed Hector Khassim! That's what I call narrowing the field. My God, haven't we got anything approaching a lead?'

Not unless the New York Police Department counted three anonymous letters accusing Palestinian terrorists, the Ambassador of Turkey and one George Nelms, plumber, of Bensonhurst.

Forty miles from New York, meanwhile, the one man who could not have killed Hector Khassim was whistling soundlessly.

'That was Huntley,' Sara yelled. 'Will you shut that thing off?'

When silence replaced the chugging whirr that had filled the barn-workshop, she began again: 'That was Huntley – '

'Our check is in the mail,' Alex interrupted regally. 'You may inform all Green Thumbs creditors that their check is in the mail.'

'Idiot,' she said fondly, perching on a nearby sawhorse. 'Who made out the checks last night?'

'You did,' said Alex graciously. 'But who walked down to the post office?'

'Two blocks,' Sara reminded him. 'Anyway, I told Huntley not to worry. I also told him that we were planning to order some more acrylic.'

'What beautiful words,' Alex murmured.

Together they looked around the barn, and together they saw the same thing. In place of the secondhand drill press, there would be brand-new industrial equipment. Instead of workbenches for two part-time men and some after-school students, there would be a modest assembly line. The sign GREEN THUMBS would continue to hang over the weathered barn, but there was plenty of room out back for a small concrete-block addition that would make up in efficiency what it lacked in picturesque charm.

'God,' said Alex expansively, 'I feel good.'

'Me too,' said Sara.

He made as if to restart the sander, then held back. 'Thanks to your father, Sara,' he said. 'He really comes through when it counts.'

This pleased Sara, as it was designed to. Turning to Paul was always harder for her than it was for Alex. Deliberately, he added, 'And the auction has really shown the world, hasn't it?'

'You saw the *Times*? Wasn't it tremendous?' she bubbled over. Despite Alex's public utterances, Parajians' size and success remained a touchy subject. Today, for example, Parke-Bernet had not yet been mentioned. 'I knew it was a superb collection but I never dreamed – '

She did not need the encouragement he had ready: 'I was holding my breath during most of the bidding.'

'It really was something!' she said, rising and brushing sawdust off her slacks. 'Daddy outdid himself this time.'

'He's a hard man to beat,' Alex agreed cordially.

'Well, you get to work. I'm going back to cut off your creditors at the pass.'

'Just watch your step,' he bellowed after her. 'If Sears, Roebuck calls with a big order, send them right out!'

Their communion was perfect, and highly selective. What Sara could not say to Alex she was telling herself as she strolled back to the house.

'The way things look, that auction is going to be more important to me and Alex than to anybody else in the family.'

She would have been surprised to learn that Alex too was guarding his tongue.

'Why the hell,' he asked himself, beveling an edge, 'did Sara and I ever pay any attention to my dear brother-in-law?'

21. The Bird is on the Wing

At the Sloan Guaranty Trust, events conspired to put Parajians on hold. The same *Times* that reviewed the auction carried a policy statement by the Chairman of the Federal Reserve Board. He was so deeply concerned about the fabric of society, he feared for Western civilization.

'Oh, Jesus!' moaned Walter Bowman. 'There go Federal Funds again!'

On the following day, the Chairman of the President's Council of Economic Advisers disclosed the cause of recession: inflation, crop failure and the Troubles in Northern Ireland. The American public, he announced peevishly, was showing an irresponsible lack of self-discipline.

Charlie Trinkam added a garnish to these funeral meats. 'The Consolidated Gas bond offering just fell flat.'

'Business loans are up five hundred million in New York,' said Everett Gabler, contributing to the tale of woe. 'What we need now ...'

Whatever they needed, they got a speech justifying wheat sales by the Secretary of Agriculture.

'Just watch T-bills now!' said Walter.

But he said it in passing. When madness hits the money markets, the voice of the politician, columnist and mutual-fund salesman is loud in the land. Bankers, especially New York City bankers, get busy.

John Thatcher was fully occupied with hour-to-hour adjustments – and so was his staff.

'We've just about finished the arrangements,' said Charlie, stifling a yawn. 'Sorry – I was up past my normal bedtime. We're ready to take over these loans from Flower State National ...'

Harassed bank presidents from Maine to Florida were pounding on the Sloan's doors and seriously disrupting Charlie's social life.

'Okay,' said the tireless Walter. 'Give me the totals, and I'll clear it with Wilcox, if he's still conscious.'

Everett presumably had no social life. 'Are you finished with Flower State, Charlie?' he inquired with meticulous regard for priority.

'Oh God, I hope so!'

'Then, John, I think we'd better scrutinize this commercial-paper debacle. At close of business yesterday –'

Everett's strong words were about to become stronger when there was an interruption.

'Yes, Miss Corsa?' Thatcher hid his irritation, although his instructions had been explicit. Miss Corsa had uncomplainingly logged so many hours of overtime she was entitled to a small lapse.

And she could scarcely be blamed for noticing Everett's scowl.

'Mrs Norris insisted,' she said.

'My Mrs Norris? Good heavens – !' Everett was half out of his chair when Miss Corsa struck again:

'She says *you* insisted.'

'We do not have unlimited time, Miss Corsa,' said Thatcher. Hoisting Everett by his own petard could take forever at this rate. 'What is the message?'

'Mrs Norris is afraid the Parajian wedding may have slipped Mr Gabler's mind. It's time for him to leave.'

With a Mona Lisa smile, she withdrew.

Everett had not only forgotten about the wedding, he had forgotten about the Parajians.

'Who hasn't?' Thatcher remarked. The auction seemed months, not days, past. 'God knows, we've got more important things to think about than Oriental rugs.'

Walter tried to help too. 'If you've got to go, you've got to go,' he said consolingly. 'Don't worry about the commercial paper. I've got that all taped and ready.'

Charlie's diagnosis differed. 'Worried about whether you're wearing the right thing, Ev? These days, anything goes,' he said, making a summer-weight business suit sound like rhinestone-studded blue jeans.

Everett was a torn man, but a promise is a promise. 'Much as I regret leaving, I believe I can turn the time to good account,' he said frugally. 'After the festivities are over, I should be able to initial their final plans for India.'

He departed for Amagansett on a wave of virtue.

'Do you think he kisses the bride?' Charlie asked the world at large.

Commendably, Bowman stuck with commercial paper. By midmorning, he, Thatcher and Charlie had done everything humanly possible to prepare the Sloan for the deluge.

'We're in pretty good shape,' said Walter, pushing back his chair. 'Some of these commitments are bigger than I want, but at least we're not mixed up with the wrong German banks, like some people I could mention.'

'We could all mention them, Walter,' said Charlie.

Was this the time to snipe at the competition? 'I'm reasonably satisfied with our position,' said Thatcher, accompanying them to the door. 'Unless, of course, one of our leaders has hurled another thunderbolt. Anything important, Miss Corsa?'

She was a fine fielder of special items on the ticker, TV news alerts and ICC leaks. Unfortunately, Miss Corsa had her idiosyncrasies.

'Mr Withers called,' she reported. 'If you're free for an early lunch, he wants very much to join you. He says it's important.'

'You'd be better off catching bouquets with Everett,' Charlie guffawed.

Walter's comfort was less fanciful. 'You said you're reasonably satisfied, John. So you can afford the time that Brad's going to waste.'

Miss Corsa pretended not to hear.

The only liquidity that engaged Bradford Withers was physical, not financial.

'... a salt-tablet dispenser beside every water fountain,' he was saying not much later. 'I've told Personnel that I'm concerned about the well-being of the staff.'

'So long as it isn't salary schedules, Brad,' Thatcher murmured without effect.

'Although that is beside the main point. In the past few days, I have been giving Sloan policy serious consideration, and I believe I see room for improvement.'

All things are possible. Perhaps Brad's unusual attendance at the Sloan had ignited a flickering interest in banking. Thatcher was cautious. 'What improvements did you have in mind?'

'Vacations,' said Withers with sublime simplicity.

Upon request, he elaborated. It had just come to his attention that most of the Sloan took its annual leave (two weeks to four weeks, with dividing lines like barbed wire) during the summer. Christmas at Kitzbühel, like Easter at Aruba, was confined to vice-presidents.

'Now, autumn and early spring are the best times to do many things, including travel. Just think of London in October.'

Was there any use telling Brad about holiday budgets, or the school year? Thatcher opted for less alien ground.

'Normally, summer is our slowest season,' he said.

'Even so, we're too rigid,' Brad shot back. 'As you know, I've been consulting with city authorities . . .'

The cloud lifted slowly. This was fallout from the Mayor's attempts to stagger Wall Street's working hours. Brad, who had never seen a rush hour in his life, was going to the heart of a different problem.

Thatcher promised to give the matter his best attention.

'I hope you will, John,' said Withers, looking around the Executive Dining Room as if he would miss it. 'I'd like to keep plugging, but as you know, we're sailing tomorrow.'

In Withers' lexicon, sailing did not refer to common carriers.

'Is it the America's Cup again?' Thatcher tried a shot at random.

No, it was not. The Witherses, together with a party of kindred spirits (and a large crew), were pushing off for the Galapagos in the eighty-foot *Carrie B.*

'Finally!' said Withers with indignation. 'Do you realize that we have been waiting *four* weeks for that auxiliary motor?'

'That long?' Contrary to expectations, Thatcher was deriving some benefit from this occasion. He already knew engine deliveries were slow all over the country. But he was glad to have Brad's presence explained. The President of the Sloan Guaranty Trust had simply been stranded ashore.

'First, they said they would ship in one week. Then it was two. Then it was four. And do you know how I got it done in the end? I went down to Annapolis myself. I always say, if you want a thing done well, do it yourself!'

This would certainly have surprised his wife, his secretary and the *Carrie B.*'s captain.

'But you're ready now?' Thatcher inquired.

'When I set my mind on something,' said Bradford Withers, 'I don't let anything stand in my way. And John, I don't want you to think this is only a mere jaunt. I expect to gather important information about the Sloan's opportunities in Ecuador!'

There was only one thing to say, and Thatcher said it: 'Bon voyage!'

Ken Nicolls was waiting for a signature when Thatcher returned to the sixth floor.

'I'm sorry to bother you, but Mr Gabler isn't in the office.'

'Probably throwing rice at the bride,' said Thatcher, scrawling. 'He went out to Amagansett to the Parajian wedding. That reminds me, did you ever get your rug?'

'I've got it narrowed down to a Basiri or an Afshar,' said Ken in a portentous voice. 'It's not the kind of thing you can make a snap decision about. I'm doing a lot of hard thinking.'

'I see,' said Thatcher, before he woke to the fact that Nicolls was hovering. 'Was there something else you wanted, Nicolls?'

Ken drew himself up. 'Mr Thatcher, I'm supposed to start my vacation on Friday. But the way things have been going for the past few days – well, I wondered if you wanted me to put it off.'

'If things were that bad,' said Thatcher, 'Gabler would not be sipping champagne at this very moment. I don't think we'll need the sacrifice.' He hoped he sounded kindly enough to rob the words of their sting. Three weeks on Cape Cod represented the Galapagos and then some to Nicolls – and Thatcher knew it.

'It wouldn't be any trouble,' Ken lied nobly.

Upstairs, the old man of the sea, weighing anchor. Here, the boy standing on the burning deck.

'Oh, go buy yourself a rug!' said Thatcher forcefully. 'Better still, make sure everything piled on your desk is cleaned up before you leave.'

Ken fled, nearly knocking Miss Corsa down in the process.

'Now what?' Thatcher was goaded.

Unfortunately, she had overheard his reference to clean desks. Her silence, as she added two inches of material to the well-packed base, was eloquent. The telephone rang just in time.

'Mr Thatcher's office ... What? I'm afraid ... I don't know if he is back yet.'

With a hand clamped over the mouthpiece, she relayed the bad news. Mr Withers wanted to speak with someone about a broken propeller.

'Tell him that I've gone out,' said Thatcher, rising hastily.

Once he was safely in the corridor, he realized he was being unfair. Everett Gabler had abandoned commercial paper to gallivant off to Long Island; Ken Nicolls was letting nine-by-twelves come between him and his obligations to the Sloan. The only adherent of business-as-usual was Bradford Withers. No one had ever claimed that his business-as-usual was banking. Like the Parajians, he was carrying on as if nothing had happened.

Unconsciously slowing his steps, Thatcher pondered this. Beyond question, something had happened to the Parajians. Their two murders were still preoccupying reporters and policemen. But in realistic terms, how significant had those deaths been? What difference had they made? Out in Amagansett, there was a wedding on the lawn. On Fifth Avenue, a salesman was diligently keeping tabs on Ken Nicolls.

After two murders even Bradford Withers, who did not let anything stand in his way, might have revised his plans.

'If you want a thing done well ...'

Thatcher came to an abrupt halt as two other presidential homilies recurred to him.

The more things change ...

Where there's a will . . .

'Good God!' he said aloud, suddenly glimpsing how these hoary maxims could forge a chain. The links of evidence were already at hand.

There were places as far apart as Teheran and Lansing, Michigan.

There were brothers with very different temperaments.

And there were too many living reminders of the past.

22. Turn Down an Empty Glass

As the rest of the sixth floor respectfully detoured around him, John Thatcher came to a sobering conclusion. He knew who had committed two murders, and he had not one particle of concrete proof. Of course, once they were headed in the right direction, the police might ultimately assemble a case compelling enough for the most exacting prosecutor. But the Parajians were destined for complex civil litigation as well. Courts do not lightly overturn property arrangements of many years' standing. Charges and countercharges would be exchanged. More than one judge and jury would be hearing foreign witnesses tell of far-off times and places. And from what he had seen of the youthful faces on recent jurors, half of them would need to have World War II explained to them.

All this would take months, if not years. And right now Everett Gabler was making God-knew-what commitments to a company on the verge of cataclysmic convulsions.

Thatcher squared his shoulders. He might be helpless to ward off all the tribulations of coming days, but one thing he could do. He could telephone Everett. Reluctantly, he visualized the scene. A telephone in the midst of a throng of guests, Everett barking questions over the strains of an orchestra, people interrupting with pieces of wedding cake.

Unnoticed, Thatcher's subconscious had been trudging along, producing one confirmation after another for his theory. There were the words of a man about to be murdered. There was the unaccountable reversal of position at a hugely successful auction. There was the final moment when the Parajians, in a rare display of unity, had toasted the success of the firm. Today, naturally, they would be toasting the bride . . .

His sudden pivot almost toppled the clerk who had been cautiously circumnavigating the obstruction in the hall.

'I beg your pardon, Miss Dewberry. Good God, what a fool I am!' he said in one breath. 'The wedding is exactly the place where I can find proof. That is, if only ...'

Without another word, he left a gaping Miss Dewberry and bolted back to his suite like a fox going to earth. Charging past Miss Corsa, he dived at her phone book, looked up the number of an obscure agency of New York City and made a long arm across her desk. Within one minute he was downing the receiver and looking around like the two-dollar bettor who has just won the daily double.

This entire performance had taken place under the coldly reproving gaze of his secretary. Motionless, she had watched one inroad on her domain after another. In grim silence she waited. A lesser woman would have folded her arms.

But there was worse to come.

'Now, Miss Corsa, there's no time to lose,' rapped out Thatcher. 'Get me a limousine right away. Then you're to call the Parajian place where they're having the wedding. Mrs Norris will know. Tell Mr Gabler that he's to stall, to temporize, to faint if he wants to. But not to agree to anything until I get there. I will join him as soon as possible.'

Miss Corsa was scandalized.

'Mr Thatcher!' she cried, appalled at the enormity he was contemplating. 'You can't go to a wedding without an invitation.'

Over the years Miss Corsa had sensed many flaws in her employer. He was prone to untimely frivolity, he had insufficient respect for his position, he was slow in taking instruction. But these were blemishes that an alert secretary could conceal from the eyes of the world. Now, apparently, he was embarking on a career as a gate-crasher.

Even as he was nerved to go over the top, Thatcher heeded the call of social propriety. Irritably he pointed to the clock.

'Amagansett is practically in Europe,' he growled. 'The wedding will be long over by the time I get there. All you have to do is make that call.'

For once, Miss Corsa quailed.

'Are you sure you wouldn't like to speak with Mr Gabler yourself?'

'*No!* I'm leaving now. Get me that limousine!'

On the endless drive to Amagansett, Thatcher had two resources besides his own thoughts. First there was the driver, pleased at this extended access to a financial man. He had, it developed, purchased his house many years ago and was the fortunate possessor of a five-and-three-quarters-percent mortgage.

'Now, that's what I call an investment,' he preened himself.

But he was worried about the broader scene. His married son had been forced to settle for an apartment.

'And what will he have to show for it after twenty years? A pile of rent receipts, that's what!'

The analysis of mortgage money, housing starts and land values that followed would have been more reassuring if it had come from Washington. Where was the country going, Thatcher wondered, when the man in the street was more knowledgeable than the satraps of the administration?

A more positive note was introduced by the second diversion, the radio. The announcer was predicting an imminent end to the heat wave now in its third day.

'A line of thundersqualls moving up the coast,' he said happily as they spiraled off the bridge onto the Brooklyn-Queens Expressway.

Thereafter their progression the length of Long Island seemed synchronized with the approaching storm.

'Over an inch of rain in Philadelphia,' the announcer reported as they zoomed into Nassau.

By the time they were shifting south to the Sunrise Highway, it was gale warnings from Eastport to Block Island. Their passage through the Hamptons was accompanied by the cheerful prediction of gusts up to seventy miles an hour with temperatures dropping into the fifties.

So neatly meshed were the two advances that Thatcher was beginning to see himself armed with Jovian thunderbolts trained on Amagansett.

But even Olympians have their qualms. When they finally pulled up to Paul Parajian's door, Thatcher was relieved to see that his calculations had been correct. The churned-up gravel driveway was testament to all the cars that had come and, mercifully, gone. The only strangers visible were employees of a catering firm, clearing up debris. One of them, armed with a spiked stick, was pursuing the crumpled napkins and cigarette packs already stirring in the rising wind. Three of them were wrestling with the poles of a marquee that had swelled with air until it looked ready for flight. And as further assurance that the festivities were over, Paul Parajian was sprawled in a rattan chair on the veranda, glass in hand, idly watching the thunderheads that were mounting on the horizon.

'Hello, Thatcher!' he called. 'Gabler said you were picking him up. He's around somewhere with Mark.'

Mounting the steps, Thatcher murmured conventional excuses. 'I realize this is an awkward time to intrude.'

'Nonsense; there's nothing going on now but a cleanup operation.' Hospitably Parajian waved to a chair. 'Rest yourself. It won't take us a minute to find Gabler. Sara will know where they've gone.'

Pleased to have a breathing spell, Thatcher put down his attaché case while Parajian plunged through a French door, calling for his daughter. He returned to find his guest looking comfortably settled.

In fact Thatcher was appreciating the accuracy of Miss Corsa's social instinct. Finding evidence was a problem he could handle; manufacturing small talk today might well prove beyond him.

Parajian gave him no time to stew in his juice. 'Gabler said you were just passing by and hoped we didn't mind if he waited for a ride,' he began deliberately. 'But then, he has always been a discreet man.'

Mentally Thatcher cursed Everett's lack of inventiveness. Only a striped bass would be just passing by Amagansett. Charlie Trinkam would have spun some flight of fancy so attractive his hearers would have suspended disbelief.

'I daresay it must seem puzzling to you,' Thatcher stonewalled.

'And it was after the call that Gabler became reluctant to finalize our arrangements about the loan. Mark was surprised. Earlier he mentioned signing everything today.'

In other words, Everett had roused suspicion on every front. What the hell, thought Thatcher. This charade had been doomed from the start. He had accomplished his two objectives, that was the important thing.

'I suppose you could say that I am on a cleanup operation myself,' he said slowly.

Parajian cocked his head, his shrewd dark eyes never leaving Thatcher's face.

'You see, I know who the murderer is. It was only a question of realizing how much alike all young Armenians looked to Americans – particularly at a time when foreigners were pouring into the country.'

'Very true.' Parajian sighed. 'I have been afraid for some time that it would have to come out. I have even occasionally thought it might be a relief for the family. Still, it is not easy for anyone to learn that he has been deceived for years and years.'

No matter what face the individual Parajians had been presenting to the outside world, Paul would not have been misled. Thatcher was certain that he knew to a millimeter which cracks were widening, which foundations were splitting. For weeks now, he must have been measuring the stresses of concealment against the strains of exposure.

But he was still not ready to let anyone else make his decision for him.

'You say you know, Thatcher. But do you have proof?'

'I will. The modern world is so filled with records, with drivers' licenses and credit cards, we forget that the older world had its records too. It is only a question of knowing what to look for.'

Thatcher was relieved that Gabler chose this moment to emerge onto the veranda.

'John, I'm glad you have arrived.'

Normally Everett would have been bursting with questions and with indignation. But not today. When John Thatcher broke all the rules, particularly in this family, he was afraid to ask anything.

And Parajian was too abstracted to play the host smoothly. 'I suppose we should have a drink. I thought I had a glass somewhere ... oh, well, never mind that now.' He had risen to his feet and was standing as if only half decided. Then he fell back on his natural bluntness.

'Thatcher has discovered who the murderer is. No doubt he will tell you all about it,' he said brusquely to Gabler before turning to Thatcher. 'I think, however, that it might be easier for everyone if I take care of the other explanations.'

And after all, thought Thatcher, why not? This had been peculiarly a family crime. Should not the accusations, the justifications, the recriminations take place within the same circle?

'Yes, that would be better for all concerned.'

'Thank you.' Parajian was already on his way indoors. Over his shoulder he said, 'You'll find Barney and Gregory in the living room.'

It took almost half an hour to satisfy Everett's curiosity, but Barney and Gregory were still there, overcome by post-wedding lassitude. Incuriously they accepted Thatcher's explanation that the Sloan wanted a final word with Paul.

'Great to have you,' Barney said automatically. 'Paul will be in soon. Don't know where he is.'

'Probably battening down the hatches. I suppose I ought to help get the stuff in from the porch,' said Gregory, without stirring. 'They say it's going to be a real boomer.'

But as the minutes lengthened into a quarter hour, and then a half hour, he began to cast puzzled glances at these stubborn guests who would not go. Even the arrival of Lois and Alex, drifting in from the lawn, did not ease the growing atmosphere of constraint.

'Well, the caterers are done,' Lois announced. 'I made them fill in the peg holes. You have to watch these people.'

'The place will look like a mess tomorrow anyway,' said Alex on general principles. 'There'll be branches down and bushes uprooted. We'll be lucky if there's power.'

Lois cast a disapproving glance through the window, where stunted trees could be seen whipping ominously in the fading light. 'Why anybody wants to live by the ocean ...' she murmured.

Already the large old summer house was beginning to creak and groan as the buffets of wind strengthened. The level of noise had been rising so imperceptibly as the storm approached that Thatcher paid no attention to the slamming door and the tramping of feet in the back hall. Right now doors were slamming everywhere, and all over the shoreline people were rushing to tie things down, bring things in and close things up.

He realized how wrong he had been when Mark, white-faced, broke into the room.

'What's going on?' he demanded. 'Paul just took his boat out – in this!'

He strode to a corner window and pointed to the Atlantic. They could all see the foaming whitecaps, the rolling swell, the looming black clouds, just visible in the deepening twilight.

'I yelled to him, but he just took off like a bat out of hell. My God, the small-craft warnings have been up for hours.'

Gregory was on his feet. 'Didn't you do anything?'

'Like what? I've called the Coast Guard, and Sara's gone up to Harriet. Do you realize he can get killed out there?'

With sinking heart, Thatcher realized he should have foreseen this. It had never occurred to him.

The bickering between the brothers came to a halt when Sara appeared in the doorway, one hand clutching the doorjamb for support.

'I don't understand,' she stammered. 'Harriet wasn't surprised. She says she's been afraid of something like this ever since Daddy told her.'

Alex had started toward his wife, but Sara was looking at Mark and Gregory. 'Oh, Gregory, then she started to cry and said maybe it was better this way. Paul could never stand prison.'

'You don't know what you're talking about,' Mark said roughly. 'And Harriet must be hysterical.' He was speaking with all the anger of a man afraid where logic would take him.

Alex understood Sara's news. 'Use your head,' he advised. 'This must mean that Paul is the murderer.'

Mark rounded on him. 'And suppose you give me one good reason why Paul would want to kill Veron! Look at your own motives.'

'Lay off!' Gregory snapped. 'It isn't Alex's fault.'

Sadly Thatcher acknowledged that he could no longer keep silent. Paul had told Harriet. It was up to him to tell the others.

'Surely,' he said as gently as he could, 'by now you must realize that the man we all knew as Paul Parajian was actually your uncle, Haig!'

23. Strange, Is It Not?

'Haig!' cried Mark. 'But Haig died before the war.'

'No,' Thatcher corrected, 'it was Paul who was killed in that accident. The seeds of two murders were planted over thirty years ago.'

Thatcher's revelation, coming hard on the heels of Sara's announcement, silenced the family. Mark closed his eyes in pain, while Sara stood frozen in the doorway.

Gregory had sunk back into his chair and was sitting with his head in his hands.

But Barney Olender was still fighting. 'I don't know what's gotten into all of you,' he said hoarsely. 'Paul scaring the daylights out of Harriet, and then you people from the Sloan with this wild story. There's never been any question that Paul's Paul. He's got to be.'

'There would have been plenty of questions if we had been thinking rationally,' Thatcher replied. 'Why was Mrs Aratounian killed almost the minute she set foot in this country? At first we all thought that a false Veron couldn't stand up to prolonged contact with Paul. But when her identity was verified, we went on to different theories. Instead, we should have stayed right there and concluded that a false Paul could not deceive his sister very long.'

'But Daddy was the one who wanted her to come,' Sara said. 'We objected, but he was all for it. Why should he insist if he was afraid of her?'

'He was by no means insistent. Once he had to deal with a *fait accompli*, he put a good face on it. But look at his behavior before then.'

Everett Gabler coughed precisely. 'He certainly placed no impediment in the way of her coming, John.'

'Everett, all the important aspects of this case have passed without mention. Almost the first thing you told me about the Aratounian troubles was that Veron had lost her last Russian relative a year earlier. And when she turned up in Teheran, everyone was surprised. In other words, Paul Parajian, the apostle of family feeling, the brother who had been very close to Veron, had not invited her to come.'

Gabler blinked. 'Parajian said he was considering it.'

'When such a statement could no longer do any harm,' Thatcher said dryly. 'And how did he act after she arrived in Iran? First a nursing home, then a delay for Khassim's schedule. Everybody said he was bending over backwards in Veron's behalf. Even if that were true, it left questions. Why didn't he fly over and escort her himself? This was not a repetition of 1948, when travel was difficult and it was imperative to get the children out of their war-torn background as rapidly as possible.'

'He telephoned her,' Mark said dully. 'Almost every other day. He wasn't avoiding her.'

'He had nothing to fear but personal contact. He had been writing to her for years.'

Alex Daniels was unusually diffident as he hitched himself forward. 'Maybe it's not my place to say so, but it doesn't add up. Why the masquerade in the first place? Did it make any difference whether it was Paul or Haig who died in 1939?'

'In business matters it did.' Thatcher was now on home ground. 'Paul Parajian started his company as a one-man enterprise. He didn't have any money when his brother joined him, so he gave Haig some stock. But he did not change the nature of the company. Why should he? They were both in their twenties and thought they had plenty of time.'

'Young people constantly make that mistake,' Gabler said severely. 'Accidents can happen to anyone, and youth is no excuse for failing to regularize one's affairs.'

By sheer habit Gabler's gaze roved the room, seeking delinquents without proper wills and estate plans.

'Yes, yes.' Thatcher hastened to avoid diversion. 'But the result of this informality was that Paul Parajian had sole signing authority. The two brothers had invested everything in one bold stroke – a shipment of rugs from the Near East just before war broke out. What was Haig to do when he learned of his brother's death? The rugs were on their way, and the opportunity could never be recreated. On the spur of the moment, probably on his way to the morgue, he decided that Haig would be the one who had died. A few forgeries would take him through the formalities of acquiring the rugs.'

Lois chose this moment to exercise her talent for saying the wrong thing. 'It's perfectly clear what he was after,' she explained to all of them. 'He was simply stealing the company.'

Thatcher was not the only one who regarded her with distaste. 'There was no company to steal in those days,' he said frigidly. 'There was nothing but an inspired guess. And remember how the situation must have looked to him. Back in Greece there was a grandmother taking care of three small children. It was his duty to do the best he could for them. He had to keep money flowing back home, he had to make enough to bring everyone to New York. He could not foresee that the length and violence of the war were going to leave him with a whole new ball game.'

'You make it sound easy to swap identities that way,' Alex objected. 'But there's more to it than signing a receipt. Hell, Gregory couldn't take over Mark's identity tomorrow without being spotted by a whole raft of people.'

'Mark has an established personality and position. Bear in mind that we are talking about the late thirties when thousands of refugees were pouring into the city.' Thatcher wondered if he could describe that era for anybody who had not experienced it. 'Most Americans saw two young foreigners, speaking with the same strange accent, looking a great deal alike and working together. It was the similarities between the two that were noticed, not the differences. In many places they would be known simply as those Parajian boys.'

Alex shook his head stubbornly. 'I still say it would have been hard.'

'It was. And the actions Haig took in 1939 to avoid pitfalls ultimately provided me with a major clue. You see, I was bothered by the lack of change in the Parajian family. Murders are normally committed in order to achieve some goal. But after two deaths, there seemed to be no significant alteration in anyone's circumstances. Nobody was suddenly richer, nobody was enabled to escape an intolerable situation, nobody was effecting a transformation in life-style.'

Mark was recovering from his stupor. 'I don't see what that proves against Paul,' he said combatively. 'Hell, it doesn't prove anything at all!'

'No, but I had begun a suggestive line of thought. I couldn't find anything after Veron's death or after Khassim's. Quite suddenly I realized that if I went further back, I would have a remarkable sequence of events. It was Mr Olender who brought them to my attention.'

'Me?' Barney Olender sat bolt upright and looked imploringly around the room. 'I didn't tell him a thing, honest to God!'

'You told me about the beginning of your connection with Parajians,' Thatcher reminded him.

'Well, there wasn't any harm in that. I must have told that story a hundred times.'

'Not in the context of two murders,' Thatcher said sadly. 'If I was looking for changes, the death of Haig Parajian had produced them in abundance. Immediately afterwards, the so-called Paul moved from where he had been living, gave up his old job, disappeared into a defense factory and took on a new assistant. If it was surprising that the assistant should be a professional musician with no knowledge of rugs or Near Easterners, it was astonishing how he used that assistant. To this day, I am informed, Paul Parajian is in the habit of presiding over all important sales in the showroom. What's more, he enjoys doing it.'

Alex Daniels was frowning in thought. 'Why shouldn't he? If Green Thumbs is ever a big success, with droves of salesmen, Sara and I will still want to be on hand for the big deals.'

'A very natural feeling,' Thatcher agreed. 'But when the renowned Admiral Christiansen was willing to buy some of the first imports, who went out to Michigan to bargain? The new assistant. There had to be a compelling reason which prevented Paul Parajian from savoring that moment of triumph. And there was. Christiansen had known both brothers, and could distinguish them. The fake Paul could not really associate with anyone in the rug business. That was why Mr Olender was so essential. He brought those rugs through customs, he dealt with buyers, in fact, he became the front man. The next step was inevitable. As Mr Olender told us, Paul Parajian left his business and enlisted in the army.'

'I should have cut my tongue out!' cried Olender.

'Oh, Barney!' It was Sara, moving swiftly forward to sit on the arm of his chair. 'It wasn't your fault. How could you know?'

But Barney, the eternal gallant who should have been squeezing her hand and patting her shoulder, paid no attention. He was huddled into his own misery, staring straight ahead.

Moved by his wretchedness, Thatcher tried to minimize Barney Olender's contribution.

'Of course, these details were unnecessary. As soon as the possibility of a switch by Haig came to mind, corroboration appeared on every side – his physical vigor, according more with a man of sixty-five than with one of seventy, his inability to use a floor shift when he was supposed to have driven taxis before the war. That period in the army was his salvation. Not only did it remove the new Paul Parajian from New York for several years, it transformed him. The combination of maturity and Americanization was all that he needed. No one was surprised that he was altered, both physically and temperamentally. Even Khassim never questioned the change from the cautious, worried boy he had known. And I do not think we should forget the use to which he put his newfound prosperity. The first thing he did was institute an unremitting search for his brother's children.'

'No one is in any danger of forgetting it,' snapped Mark.

'But after finding you, he had a problem. At the time he assumed his brother's identity, he probably considered it a short-term expedient. A year would pass, he would bring the family over, then explain to his mother. Instead, he had created a whole new personality, a whole new company, and found himself faced with children too young or too sick to be burdened with any worries. So he decided to go on playing his role – until this summer.'

Alex groaned. 'He was so damned confident, he probably forgot he was playing a role.'

'He was being a damned good father to us, if that's what you mean!' Mark made it sound like a challenge. But when Alex refused to be provoked, he flung himself over to the corner window and stood with his back to the room, staring into the glass, which was now a black mirror. The rising storm could be heard and felt, but it could no longer be seen. Suddenly he drew the curtains with one savage jerk and wordlessly returned to his chair.

There was nothing to say. The only news would be tragic news. Thatcher hurried into speech to banish the silence of tortured waiting.

'In any event, Paul Parajian was forced to remember his predicament when this summer rolled around. I do not think he was worried by the conflict over company policy, even though it was the first time the three of you had united against him. Given time, I am sure he was confident he could reassert his authority with some splendid coup, such as the auction. But then Veron emerged, and he knew he was not going to get that time. We don't know much about Veron, but enough to understand his reasoning.'

Conscious of a file that would have shamed the CIA, the FBI and Dun & Bradstreet, Everett was reproachful. 'We know quite a good deal, John.'

'All right, call it a good deal. We know that she was very close to her brother Paul, she was not overly fond of her brother Haig and she had old-fashioned views about the head of the family. We can also deduce that she was an intransigent woman, capable of defeating a Russian emigration officer and an Iranian policeman. Her brother knew her better than we do, and he assumed that she would not cooperate with him. Moreover, he was being assailed by another uncompromising woman. His children had tacitly appointed his daughter-in-law leader of the opposition. She complained he was taking too much money out of the business, she thought he should be forcibly retired, she probably made his blood run cold by raising the cry of impostor. How in the world would she react if his trickery were exposed?'

Lois lifted her chin. 'I don't see why you're all looking at me that way. Naturally it would have been very unpleasant, and we would have consulted our lawyers. But I can't understand why that would have been so awful.'

'That's because you're not acquainted with the law of trusts. When Paul Parajian appropriated the stock belonging to his nephews and niece in 1939, he assumed the liabilities of a trustee. In other words, every single penny generated by that original stock is, in law, the property of the rightful owners. Your uncle owed the three of you vast sums of money, including a good deal which he had already spent.'

'But that's just plain silly!' Mark burst out. 'Paul built Parajians out of thin air.'

'Exactly. In the beginning he took over eighty-five percent of nothing. At the end of thirty years, his skill and daring had parlayed nothing into a million-dollar business with a worldwide reputation.'

Mark spread his hands helplessly. 'Why not just tell us? We would have seen his point of view.'

'It was a bad time for him to believe that. Furthermore, I think you still have not grasped some of the implications of his situation. He was not a man who had married twice and had four children. He was a man with one wife and one son. When it came to a crisis, he was not willing to undermine their position. I think it was very important to him that his son follow him at Parajians. In a court case, he might have lost everything he owned.'

Gregory was at last showing signs of coming to life. He abandoned his study of the floor and leaned back, sighing heavily. 'It was more than that. It was pride too. He was used to laying down the law all these years. He wasn't going to end up by begging.'

That made sense to Thatcher. 'You may well be right. For whatever reasons, he decided to continue as he was, even if that meant killing his sister. But he must have been appalled by the consequences. He had never contemplated a police case. Veron was supposed to lie down after lunch and die. Then the family doctor would have been called. He would have heard a multitude of witnesses describe nursing homes, jet fatigue and over-excitement. He would no doubt have signed the death certificate. But Veron made the most of her last opportunity to be refractory and insisted on going to the Sloan. Before Paul knew it, his family was embroiled in a murder investigation. Even so, he might have pulled it off.'

'If Hector had just kept his big fat nose out of it,' Gregory said viciously.

Sara was looking at him with sudden certainty. 'That's why you haven't been saying anything. You're not really surprised,' she charged. 'You've known all along.'

'Not all along. I'd just figured it out that day we had lunch at La Cheminée. It was drilling a hole in me, and I wanted to talk about it. But then I realized the only way you keep a secret is not to tell anyone.'

'It was Khassim's pictures, I suppose,' Thatcher guessed. 'I didn't understand their significance until after I'd established Paul as the murderer. But you, naturally, had a special reason to notice.'

'What's so special about Gregory?' asked Mark. 'I saw those pictures for years, and I still don't know what you're talking about.'

'That was partly your trouble,' Thatcher replied. 'Gregory was too young to remember Greece. He looked at those pictures as if for the first time.'

'So what? They were the kind you find in any family album.'

Gregory was holding out both his hands as if they were objects for sale. 'Left-handedness, Mark,' he said. 'I can't help being aware of it.'

'Veron's presence in those pictures was accidental,' Thatcher amplified. 'Actually, they were four pictures of Paul and Haig, proving that Paul was left-handed and Haig, right-handed.'

'Don't you remember Veron talking about it?' Gregory seemed to feel that it was very important. 'At the time I didn't pay much attention. I thought she meant me when she described Grandmother slapping and scolding. It was true enough, but how could Veron know? She was in Russia when I was turning out to be a leftie. She was describing the fuss about her brother in their childhood. I didn't catch on when she quoted that proverb "like parent, like child," even though she'd made it clear she wasn't interested in my daughters. She wasn't talking about me as a father, she was talking about me as a son. God, it stood out a mile once your eyes were opened. I didn't see how you could all miss it at the auction, when Paul gave us that toast. He was standing in exactly the same position as in that wedding picture – except that it was a mirror image. When you're raising a full glass of champagne, you automatically use the hand with the most control.'

Mark was beginning to understand many things that had confused him. 'Is that why nobody could find you for a couple of days before the auction?'

'Yes, I was running around like a chicken with its head cut off. At first I had some crazy idea about proving I was wrong. I was going to go to the army and find out if Paul's left hand had been injured. I was going to find someone in the rug business who'd known both Parajians when they started up. But the more I thought about it, the more I realized my suspicions were right. I wasn't going to find any evidence, and I might make things worse looking for some.'

Gregory's voice died away, even though he obviously had more to say. Finally he clenched his jaw and spoke directly to Thatcher. 'And that means you've still got some explaining to do. Once Khassim was dead, there weren't any connecting links left between Paul's two lives. I don't see how you could produce anything that would stand up in a court of law. But I'd hate to think that Paul took that boat out just because he thought we were too weak to stand the pressure.'

Thatcher had seen this moment coming for some time. 'No, you can rest easy on that score. He was genuinely concerned about the tensions you were all undergoing, but that wasn't what made him do it. Before coming out here today I called the Hack Bureau and learned that they still have the fingerprints of taxicab drivers licensed in the thirties.'

'So that was it.' Gregory nodded to himself. 'And you thought you could get some current prints to compare against the old ones?'

'The first thing I did on your porch was to put Paul Parajian's glass in my attaché case. The Sloan cannot afford – '

The shrilling of the phone interrupted Thatcher. As the strident clamor sounded, he could not have completed his sentence if his life had depended on it.

Strangely motionless, Mark licked dry lips. 'I gave the Coast Guard this number.'

Sara looked blindly at her husband and then hurled herself into his arms.

It was Gregory who heaved himself to his feet. 'I'll go,' he said. 'And then I'll tell Harriet.'

They could hear him crossing the hall, closing a door behind him.

Tautly Alex cleared his throat and spoke over his wife's head. 'So when Khassim said they weren't such old friends as he had thought, he was speaking literally. He had never really known Haig in the old days.'

'Yes,' Thatcher said, seconding Daniels' effort to keep the conversation going. 'Once Khassim tumbled to the left-handedness, I expect other memories stirred into life.'

'And he flew back to New York to talk to Paul.'

'Blackmail,' muttered Mark.

Thatcher recalled the Iranian, his ambition, his view of himself as part of Parajians. 'I'm sure he didn't think of himself as a blackmailer. He thought of himself as a close associate, who was going to become closer.'

There had been an unnatural interval after each speech as everybody in the room strained to hear. Now there was movement in the hall. Gregory had left the phone and was going upstairs, very slowly.

'Bad news,' murmured Alex Daniels.

With a flash of his old pride, Barney Olender fired up. 'What did you expect?' he asked almost tearfully. 'When Paul sets out to do something, he doesn't stop halfway.'

He was quite right, as Gregory confirmed when he returned ten minutes later. 'The Coast Guard cutter found Paul's boat capsized. They circled for a while, but it's hopeless on a night like this. They don't think chances of recovering the body are good.'

Sara mastered her distress. 'How is Harriet? Does she want me?'

'No, she says she wants to be alone for a while.' Gregory drifted over to the fireplace instead of returning to his chair. Setting his shoulders against the mantelpiece, he faced Thatcher. 'I stopped at your attaché case on my way back. That glass isn't going to be much use to you anymore.'

Alex sucked in his breath. 'You mean you wiped it?'

'Well, somebody had to,' Gregory said impatiently. 'Harriet tells me the last thing Paul did was clean up his bathroom and dressing table. We don't have to worry about the rest. There have been over a hundred people tramping through this afternoon.'

Lois stared at him as if he had gone mad. 'Didn't you understand a word of what Mr Thatcher was saying? With that glass we could have taken over the company. We may never have any other proof.'

'Shut up, honey,' he said in a voice of absent authority that nobody had ever heard him use to his wife before – except, apparently, Lois. She made no protest as he continued. 'Haven't you figured out why I kept my mouth shut? I don't know how I'd face up to murder, but I'm sure of one thing. If I'd been in his shoes, I would have done exactly what Paul did in 1939. And I can only hope to God that I'd have acted the same in 1948.'

As Gregory looked at his wife, his lips twisted into a half smile. 'It wouldn't have been easy to go scouring the DP camps for a bunch of half-savage kids – not in the first year of a happy marriage. But I like to think I would have done it, just like Paul.'

Whatever communication was taking place between the couple was remarkably effective, because Lois then stunned her husband's family by gulping audibly and saying with every appearance of sincerity, 'And I hope I would have behaved as well as Harriet.'

Gregory's smile spread across his entire face. 'You know, Veron wasn't the only Parajian who ran true to form, right up to the end. I figure that Paul was backing his judgement for the last time today. He was leaving the decision to us.'

'So without bothering to consult Sara or me,' said Mark, 'you decided to give him his way.'

'Any objections?'

Mark reddened, but did not hesitate. 'Of course not,' he said gruffly.

'Sara?'

The terse question caught her by surprise. She began to babble feverishly. 'I always thought that Green Thumbs ... I mean, without more money ... What am I saying? No, of course not.'

'All right, then, that takes care of the past,' Gregory said robustly. 'Paul was the man he always said he was. This business about Haig is just a pipe dream. Harriet and Steve inherit his interest, and the Sloan can lump it.'

Did Gregory realize he was unconsciously reaching for his father's cigar box? Thatcher thought not. In the years to come, Gregory was going to look and sound more and more like Paul.

'Now we have to think about the future of Parajians,' he said, beginning the process. 'I'm going to have to spend a lot of time on the Indian expansion, which means we'll have a manpower problem.'

'India?' Understandably, Mark was having trouble keeping pace. 'Are we still going through with that?'

'When we can get in on the ground floor, and make sure of a source for quality rugs? We'd be crazy not to!'

Mark had begun to catch up. 'Then I'll tell you one thing. Now that Stephen's become a partner, he'd better stop wasting time on camps. I'll take him with me on my buying trip next summer. He's not too young to start training his eye and learning the ropes.'

'Good! Because you and I are going to have to spend more time in the showroom, supplying the Parajian presence. I may try using Arthur Sourian in the wholesaling end. He's really wasted on the floor. Then, we'll see how things go. Sara and Alex may have to come into the business. The West Coast is getting so big it really needs ...'

*

Fifteen minutes later Thatcher and Gabler were in the limousine, their departure almost unnoticed by the Parajians. Everett, engrossed in a vision of the past, was blind to the rain streaming down the windows and deaf to the banshee wail of the wind.

'John,' he said, having difficulty getting the words out, 'do you realize that I have spent my entire professional life administering the testamentary trust of a man who was alive?'

But Thatcher had his own vision. 'Forget the past,' he advised. 'Think of the future. Parajian must have made some provision, if he died while his son was still a minor.'

Instinctively, Everett responded to the call of duty. 'He appointed the Sloan trustee for Stephen.'

'I was afraid of that. And anything could happen to the boy.'

Thatcher could see a teen-aged boy, no doubt dark, thin and cautious. He could see a plane going down in the wilds of Afghanistan. And twenty years later, he could see a bronzed stranger presenting himself at the doors of the Sloan.

'Well, by now, we've taken the measure of this family.' Thatcher was clinical. 'We've seen a daughter-in-law challenge an aunt, a father turn out to be an uncle and the whole tribe conspiring to rob themselves. When you deal with the Parajians, you have to enlarge your definition of contingencies. We're going to beat them at their own game. Before that boy goes anywhere, I want you to get his fingerprints into our files.'

Gabler had still not learned his lesson. 'How do you expect me to do that? We can't start treating the Sloan's clients like criminals.'

Thatcher was not an executive for nothing.

'I have every confidence that you will find a way. Not for a moment am I advocating that we make a habit of stealing glassware. But, Everett . . .'

An appropriate clap of thunder punctuated his final comment.

'Get those fingerprints – by hook or by crook!'

More about Penguins and Pelicans

Penguinews, which appears every month, contains details of all the new books issued by Penguins as they are published. From time to time it is supplemented by *Penguins in Print*, which is our complete list of almost 5,000 titles.

A specimen copy of *Penguinews* will be sent to you free on request. Please write to Dept EP, Penguin Books Ltd, Harmondsworth, Middlesex, for your copy.

In the U.S.A.: For a complete list of books available from Penguins in the United States write to Dept CS, Penguin Books, 625 Madison Avenue, New York, New York 10022.

In Canada: For a complete list of books available from Penguins in Canada write to Penguin Books Canada Ltd, 2801 John Street, Markham, Ontario L3R 1B4.

Emma Lathen

The Longer the Thread

Sloan were backing Slax, the sportswear manufacturers, to the tune of 3,000,000 dollars.
They had no intention of subsidizing sabotage, kidnapping, arson, murder and a political crisis.

Fortunately, there was more than a sporting chance that John Putnam Thatcher would restore the balance.

Sweet and Low

'Wit, humour and wry allusions a-plenty as John Putnam Thatcher "steps springily from the frying pan into the fire". A newly-appointed Trustee of the Leonard Dreyer Trust, Thatcher, aided and abetted by Charlie Trinkham, solves the mystery of the murders rocking the huge Dreyer Chocolate Company which brings the Trust its money. Splendidly varied entertainment' – Edmund Crispin in the *Sunday Times*

'Of the true, intelligent detective story, Emma Lathen is probably now the only competent proponent' – *The Times Literary Supplement*

Emma Lathen

When in Greece

The Sloan Guaranty Trust, the world's third largest bank, invested in a hydro-electric project in the Greek mountains.

During the Colonels' coup the Sloan's representative, Ken Nicholls, gets arrested at Salonika railway station.

A second Sloan man, Everett Gabler, is sent to retrieve him – but hasn't a chance – he is arrested too, within hours of his arrival and in broad daylight.

Against all advice, John Putnam Thatcher, the bank's vice-president, sets out for Greece and, with the help of two female archaeologists, pulls off the biggest coup of all...

Murder Without Icing

Wall Street + Ice Hockey = PR bonus for Sloan
New York Huskies – Star = dead loss

Urbane intellect × imperturbability =
John Putnam Thatcher = Solution

'There's scarcely a page that is not sheer unadulterated delight' – *Daily Telegraph*